Carisbrooke Abbey

AMANDA GRANGE

ROBERT HALE · LONDON

© Amanda Grange 2003
First published in Great Britain 2003

ISBN 0 7090 7404 2

Robert Hale Limited
Clerkenwell House
Clerkenwell Green
London EC1R 0HT

2 4 6 8 10 9 7 5 3 1

Typeset in 11/16pt Revival Roman by
Derek Doyle & Associates, Liverpool.
Printed in Great Britain by
St Edmundsbury Press, Bury St Edmunds, Suffolk.
Bound by Woolnough Bookbinding Limited

For Chris

CHAPTER ONE

Which way do I go?

Miss Hilary Wentworth, diminutive in her poke bonnet and dark-grey pelisse, peered through the steadily falling rain. The road forked ahead of her but neither direction looked inviting. To her left the road wound up the side of a hill, and to her right it disappeared into a dense wood.

She would have to examine the letter, but if she took it out of her pocket where she stood the wind would whip it out of her hand. She glanced towards the trees. Once beneath their thickly-needled branches she would have some shelter from the elements. Gripping her portmanteau tightly in one hand and holding on to her bonnet with the other she hurried towards them. Not much further . . . . Soon the first trees closed around her and the wind was held at bay. It still moaned but the further she went, the less powerful it became.

She set down her portmanteau and drew a crumpled piece of paper out of her pocket.

3 November 1810

Dear Mr Wentworth, she read.

She felt a twinge of guilt as she read the name but she hurriedly

7

went on, her eyes travelling down the page.

. . . *I am prepared to offer you the position . . . the starting salary will be . . .*

She skimmed on, until she reached the relevant passage at the bottom.

. . .*take the stagecoach . . . then a short walk . . .*

Short walk, she thought with a shake of her head, as she felt the blisters rising on her heels.

. . . *turn left at the milestone . . .*

Ah! Now she was coming to it.

. . . *and then take the road that leads . . .*

The trees stirred overhead . . . and a large splat of rain fell on to the paper, smudging the writing. She scrubbed desperately at the page, but it was too late. The water had dissolved the ink. She let out a cry of exasperation. Now how was she to find her way to the abbey?

Having given vent to her feelings she folded the letter and tucked it back in her pocket. She looked both forward and back. Ahead of her, the road passed through the trees and then emerged into the gloomy daylight, where it appeared to be straight and flat. Behind her, after leaving the trees, it wound up the hill. In the absence of any certain knowledge she decided to take the easier route. Encouraging herself with thoughts of sitting in front of a roaring fire when she finally reached the abbey, she picked up her portmanteau and continued on her way.

The storm intensified and thunder rumbled overhead. She looked up apprehensively. The trees, which had seemed sheltering, now seemed menacing. If the storm broke she would be trapped beneath them. She quickened her pace. Another rumble of thunder reverberated around her as she left the shelter of the wood, and she was hit by the full force of the storm. She clutched at her bonnet and then leant forward to fight the wind.

A minute later there was a tremendous crack! and a brilliant flash lit the sky, followed by an ominous creaking. Looking back, she saw that one of the trees had been struck by lightning . . . and it was falling towards her.

'Oh, no!'

She began to run, but not fast enough. With a loud splintering noise the tree toppled to the ground. It caught her a glancing blow as it fell, and she was knocked from her feet, her portmanteau flying out of her hand.

She lay where she fell, too dazed to move. Then, bit by bit, she began to recover from the shock and she tried to get up. But as soon as she moved she was hit by a wave of pain, and realized that the tree had landed across her ankle.

She sank back. But not for long. She knew she must make another effort, for if she stayed where she was she would catch her death of cold. She tried to sit up again, this time more cautiously. At last she was able to accomplish it, but she could see no way to free her foot.

She examined the tree. It was only the feathery branches at the top that were pinning her ankle, and she thought she might be able to lift them clear. She reached out and tried to pull them aside, but with little success: she was at an awkward angle, and could not use any leverage. Allowing herself a short rest, she tried again. She was just about to grasp one of the branches for another effort when a dark shadow fell across her. Looking up, she gasped. A large, bulky shape was standing there. It was huge and shaggy, some kind of wild animal . . . a bear, rearing up on its hind legs! Shocked, she tried to struggle free. Until another flash of lightning lit the scene, and she saw that the dark shape was not a bear at all, but a man.

Of course! There were no bears in England, she chided herself. But she could be forgiven for her mistake. He was tall and broad, and with his grizzled hair he looked wild and savage.

'Hell's teeth!' he ground out. 'What are you doing in the wood?'

His ungracious words dispelled the last traces of her fear, and stung her to make a sharp retort. 'That is none of your business.'

'Oh, isn't it?' he growled.

'No, it is not.' Focusing on her anger, which helped her to take her mind from the pain, she went on, 'So if you would just help me to free my foot—'

'Oh! So *that* is my business,' he returned churlishly.

'You are right, it isn't,' she said, biting her lip. 'Very well, then, if you are not going to make yourself useful, you had better be on your way.'

'Harumph!'

The sound came out gruffly, but another flash of lightning tore open the sky, and to Hilary's surprise she saw that there was a glint of respect in his eye. Her spirited retort had done her no harm with him, it seemed, and she was grateful. She had spoken without thinking, and it would have been disastrous if he had taken her at her word.

He turned his attention away from her and fixed it on the tree. After examining it for a few minutes he bent down and took hold of the crown. Then, flexing his huge shoulders, he lifted it from the ground.

Hilary seized the moment and pulled her foot free. She ought to thank him, but he had helped her with such a bad grace that she was reluctant to do so. Good breeding got the better of her baser instincts, however, and she muttered an unwilling, 'Thank you.'

'Don't mention it.'

And why was he so bad-tempered? she wondered, hearing his gruff tone. It wasn't as though *he* had spent the last hour tramping through the rain, trying to find an elusive abbey, and had then been knocked down by a tree!

But whatever the reason, it was not her concern. She had other things to worry about.

She turned her attention back to her foot. It was difficult to see how badly it had been injured. The lightning had retreated and the stormy day was once more dark, but her ankle was sore and it was starting to throb.

The bear-like man crouched down in front of her. Before she could stop him, he lifted her foot on to his knee. She winced, expecting him to hurt her, but his touch was strangely gentle. Though his hands were large they possessed a delicacy she had not expected. His fingers were long and broad, she noticed, and they were weatherbeaten, showing the brown hue of a man who spent much of his life out of doors. As he ran his hands over her kid boot, searching it deftly for a sign of any broken bones, to her surprise she felt her foot began to tingle. It was an unusual sensation, and yet pleasant. Better still, it seemed to blot out the pain.

She raised her eyes and in the stormy gloom she took in his face. It was strongly moulded, with powerful features. It was not handsome. Despite the charcoal eyes that pooled beneath lowering brows, it could almost have been called ugly. His nose was crooked, his jaw large, and there were two scars above his left eye.

Her gaze passed on to his hair. Its grizzled hue intrigued her. Though he was not an old man, in fact she would not have thought him above thirty, it was flecked with silver at the temples. What kind of anguish could have caused his hair to grey so young? she wondered. But then chided herself a moment later for reading too much into it. Grey hair was probably no more than a family trait.

She dropped her gaze to his hands . . . and saw that they were unlacing her boot!

'No!'

She was suddenly aware that she was alone in the woods with an unknown gentleman, and that she should not be allowing him to take such a liberty. She tried to reclaim her foot, but he held on to it firmly and began to slip off her boot.

'You've taken a nasty knock,' he said with a darkling look. 'Your ankle could be sprained.'

'It isn't,' she said quickly, snatching it back with a shiver. 'It's nothing, I assure you. It is only bruised.' She re-tied her laces with small, deft fingers and then said hurriedly, 'If you will just help me up I will be on my way.'

As soon as she had finished, she was uncomfortably aware that her brusqueness had been rude, particularly as he was trying to help her. But his presence unsettled her. The way he had made her foot feel when he had taken it in his hands had been deeply disturbing.

She was just about to apologize for her churlishness, when he swept her off her feet and held her firmly against his massive chest!

'What are you doing?' she gasped in horror.

Cradled in his arms, she was experiencing the strangest sensations. She felt a peculiar light-headedness and her heart began to beat more quickly.

'Exactly what you asked me to do,' he returned. 'Helping you up.'

'I didn't mean you to sweep me off my feet! Put me down at once!'

He shrugged, then dropped her unceremoniously to the ground, retaining just enough control to make sure that she did not land on her injured foot.

She straightened her bonnet, then winced as she put her damaged foot to the ground.

'Aha! As I thought,' he growled. 'It's sprained. You can't walk like that. I suppose I will have to carry you.'

'You will have to do no such thing.'

He had taken hold of her arm, but she stepped back, shaking him off. The thought of him sweeping her from her feet and holding her against his broad chest again was far too perturbing.

'I am quite all right,' she went on hastily, not wanting him to know how he had made her feel. 'It was a momentary twinge, nothing more.'

Having caught a glimmer of light through the trees, she was able to make little of her injury. She had almost reached her destination, and she would be able to continue alone.

Catching the direction of her glance, he agreed with her unspoken comment. 'The rectory's only a few minutes away. You can manage it without getting into any more trouble.'

'I am not . . .' she said, turning to glance at the beckoning light, but when she looked back she found he had melted away into the trees as suddenly as he had appeared.

'Well I never!' she exclaimed.

How had he managed it? She wouldn't have believed that a man of such bulk could disappear so quickly. But he must be a forester, she reasoned, thinking of his weatherbeaten face and hands, and if so he would be used to moving swiftly and noiselessly out of doors.

She gave herself a moment to recover from the strange encounter then she bent down and picked up her portmanteau. Limping, she set off towards the light. It was slow going, and painful, but she knew that once she reached the rectory she would be able to ask for directions to the abbey. Perhaps the rector, if he was a true Christian, would offer her the use of his horse.

She bent her head against the driving rain and followed the road. Soon she came to a pleasant stone building with a small garden in front of it and a neatly painted gate. The sight reassured her. After her adventure in the woods it was good to see something so solid and normal. She hesitated for a moment before opening the gate, but the rain drove her on and before another minute had passed she was knocking on the door.

There was the sound of exclamations from inside, and hurried footsteps, then the door opened and a woman's face peered out. It was surrounded by a mob cap, from which fluffy fair hair protruded.

'Mercy me, it's a young girl!' exclaimed the woman. She opened the door wide and pulled Hilary in. 'Come in, dear,' she said, as she did so. 'Don't stand out there in the rain, or you'll be soaked.'

A loud sneeze came from the room to the left of the hall, followed by a cry of, 'Who is it . . . *a-choo!* . . . Martha?'

'It's a young woman, Obadiah. Lost her way, by the look of things. She's as wet as a mermaid, poor dear.'

The woman ushered Hilary into a snug sitting-room. It was a cosy apartment, and provided a welcome contrast to the gloomy day outside. Despite the earliness of the hour the curtains were drawn. They shut out the sight of the wind-beaten trees, which bent and twisted with every fresh blast. Even the noise was somewhat kept out by their heavy damask. The walls were painted in a warm shade of apricot, which glowed in the firelight, taking on the appearance of red gold. The ceiling was low and crossed by heavy oak beams. Their heaviness was lightened by the furniture, which was more modern in style. A sofa upholstered in gold damask was set to the left of the door, and a wing chair was placed to the right of the log fire, which filled the inglenook fireplace and sent heat into the far corners of the room.

To the left of the fire sat an elderly man with his feet in a bowl of hot water. A towel was round his shoulders, and his breeches were rolled up to his knees.

'I'm . . . *achoo!* . . . sorry to greet you like this,' said the rector, starting to rise.

'Now don't you get up, Obadiah. I'm sure the young lady will understand.' She turned to Hilary. 'Don't come too close, dear. You don't want to catch it. Here.' She pulled a chair forward for Hilary, and set it down at the other side of the fire. 'Sit down, and make yourself comfortable. We'll soon have you dry.'

'That's very kind of you,' said Hilary, 'but I cannot stay. I lost my way in the woods and I have only stopped to ask for directions.'

'Ah. You'll be wanting the village,' said the woman knowledgeably. 'You've come from over the hill, I suppose?'

'No.' Hilary shook her head, and tried to ignore the pain in her foot. 'I've come from Derbyshire. I am wanting to find the abbey.'

There was a sudden stillness in the room, and the woman's kindly face went blank.

'Carisbrooke Abbey,' Hilary elaborated.

Martha cast her husband, the rector, a quick look, and they exchanged glances.

'No, I don't think you'll be wanting the abbey,' said Martha, with a falsely cheerful air.

'Yes.' Hilary was definite. 'I have an appointment.'

Ordinarily their strange manner on hearing the abbey mentioned would have disturbed her, but at present she was too cold and wet to be troubled by it. She wanted one thing and one thing only: to reach Carisbrooke Abbey without delay.

'Well . . .'

The woman looked dubious, but her husband turned to Hilary and said, 'If you have an appointment then, of course, you must keep it. But you cannot go any further on foot. John must take you in the carriage.'

'On a night like this?' demanded his wife.

'Hush, Wife,' he said in admonishing tones.

'I don't want to be any trouble,' said Hilary. 'Perhaps if I could just borrow a horse?'

'It is John's duty as . . . *achoo!* . . . a Christian to take you,' said the rector. 'Martha, ring the bell.'

Fussing and flustering, Martha rang the bell, and before long a dour old man entered the room.

'This young lady wishes to go to the abbey, John.'

'To t'abbey?' he asked suspiciously.

'Yes, John. The abbey.'

John cast her a doubtful glance, but then shrugged, and said, 'Very good, maister,' before turning and leaving the room.

Well, his strange attitude was not to be wondered at, thought Hilary, finally realizing something was amiss. It wasn't that she had precisely lied to secure the position at the abbey, but she had not been altogether truthful either, and she doubted that anyone in the neighbourhood would be prepared for a young woman to join the staff.

'Now come and sit by the fire. You might as well get warm whilst John readies the horses,' said the rector. 'Never fear, he won't be long.'

'That's right, dear,' said Martha, all bustle once again.

She sat Hilary hospitably in front of the roaring blaze and Hilary made no further protest. She sank gratefully into the comfortable chair and stretched out her hands in front of her, warming them at the flames.

'So, you're going to the abbey,' said the rector.

'Yes.' She hesitated. 'Is it a real abbey?

'Oh, yes,' nodded the rector.

Visions of dark tombs, creaking doors and secret passages assailed Hilary's imagination. Much as she enjoyed reading about them in Mrs Radcliffe's novels, the idea of experiencing them was daunting. For a moment she wished she had not accepted the position, but as she had not been offered any other form of employment she had been driven to take it.

'Or at least, it was,' he continued, 'but when King Henry dissolved the monasteries and sold much of the church's land, it passed into secular hands.' He shook his head, as though mourning something that had happened three, instead of nearly three hundred, years ago. 'That was when Lord Carisbrooke bought it – the first Lord Carisbrooke that is, the present Lord Carisbrooke's ancestor.'

Hilary leant back in her chair. She could feel her injured foot

starting to swell and press against the inside of her boot. She longed
to remove it, but for the moment it was not possible.

'And he, of course, turned it into his residence,' said the rector.

The door opened and John entered the room.

'All ready, John?' asked the rector.

John tugged his forelock. 'Aye, maister.'

'Good.' He turned to Hilary. 'Then we mustn't keep you.'

Hilary stood up. 'Thank you for the use of your carriage, and the
use of your fire,' she said gratefully. 'I really do appreciate it.'

She picked up her portmanteau and Martha showed her to the
door. As she climbed, with some difficulty, into the carriage, Martha
waved her off and then John closed the door. Leaning back against
the squabs, Hilary felt a momentary qualm as she thought of what
was to come, but she told herself not to be so cowardly. She had
come this far: she would see it through.

There was a jolt, and the carriage pulled away. Rain thrummed on
the roof and bounced from the puddles as John manoeuvred it carefully down the road, continuing in the direction Hilary had been
heading. As the minutes passed she was more and more thankful
that she had found the rectory. The abbey was evidently still some
way away and she would have been exhausted by the time she had
reached it if she had had to continue on foot.

At last, the carriage turned to the left, and Hilary leaned forward.

Peering out of the window she could see little through the curtain
of rain, but by and by some dim lights showed in the distance and
she saw the bulk of a large building outlined against the sky. So this
was to be her new home – if her luck held, that was.

The carriage rumbled to a halt. John climbed down from the box
and opened the door, and Hilary stepped out.

Seen beneath the black sky, which had turned the November
afternoon into something resembling night, the abbey was not a
welcoming sight. Its Gothic architecture was gaunt, with jagged

spires reaching into the sky. Flying buttresses supported its walls and tall, narrow windows lined its sides. Before her was an arched door made of solid oak, set in a surround of heavily carved stone. Above it was a rose window. The window should have been beautiful, but instead it was forbidding. It reminded Hilary of a huge eye, watching her.

But she was being fanciful. Besides, there was no turning back; she must do what she had come to do.

Steeling her nerve, she went up the steps to the front door. It was enormous, and she felt tiny standing in front of it. She fought down a frisson of fear, then straightening her pelisse, she lifted the heavy iron knocker and let it fall. A loud clanging noise reverberated through the gloomy afternoon. By and by, the noise died away. No one came. She waited. Still no one came. She raised the knocker and was just about to let it fall again when she heard shuffling footsteps approaching the other side of the door. There was the sound of bolts being drawn back, and then the door creaked open.

An ancient butler, bent and crooked, stood there. He was dressed all in black. To Hilary's overstretched nerves he looked like a bird of ill omen.

He bent forward and peered at her insolently.

'What do you want?' he asked suspiciously.

'I am here to see Lord Carisbrooke,' she said politely.

'His lordship don't want to see the likes of you.'

She was taken aback by his rudeness, but quickly recovering herself, she said firmly, 'I have an appointment.'

A pleasant gentlemanly voice called from somewhere behind the door. 'If the lady has an appointment, Lund, you had better let her in.'

Lund gave Hilary a sour look. Then he stood aside.

Hilary, summoning her courage, stepped over the threshold. She found herself in a cavernous stone-flagged hall. Suits of armour glinted in the shadows under the staircase, which rose in a sweep of stone from the corner of the hall before finally disappearing into the darkness above, and large tapestries hung on the walls.

A huge fireplace dominated the hall. It was flanked by two oak tables on which large branched candelabras were set, but their flickering flames, even when mixed with the leaping flames of the log fire, could not illuminate the corners of the massive space.

Above the fireplace was a fearsome-looking collection of weapons. Two-handed swords and heavy maces were mixed with spears and axes, interspersed with battered shields.

Hilary shivered. It was not a welcoming place.

But the sight of an amiable-looking gentleman standing in front of the fireplace with a large hound lying at his feet did much to dispel her forebodings. He had a handsome face and graceful posture, and was elegantly dressed. His cravat was arranged with precision, and there were frills of lace at his cuffs. His blue tailcoat was well cut, and his breeches were pulled smoothly over his slender legs.

'My dear young lady, you are drenched,' the gentleman said. 'Do come over here and take a seat by the fire.'

Hilary was unwilling to impose on his hospitality and felt she must inform him of her status immediately.

'That is very kind of you, Lord Carisbrooke, but I feel I should introduce myself. I—'

'Lord Carisbrooke?' His face broke into a charming smile. 'I'm afraid you are under a misapprehension. I am not Lord Carisbrooke.'

'No?' Hilary was surprised.

His smile became rueful. 'Unfortunately not.'

'Oh.'

Hilary was disappointed. She was sure he would have honoured her appointment, if he had been the earl.

'But perhaps I can be of assistance? I am his cousin – his distant cousin. My name is Ulverstone.'

'Mr Ulverstone.' Hilary inclined her head.

She was just about to explain her presence when the door, caught by a gust of wind, banged open. She started, then looked towards it . . . and felt a sinking sensation in the pit of her stomach. For there, standing in the doorway was the broad-shouldered, shaggy-haired, bear-like figure she had met in the woods.

'That won't be necessary,' he growled.

'Ah, Marcus, there you are.' The elegant young gentleman's eyes twinkled. 'You did not tell me you were expecting such delightful company.'

Marcus, Lord Carisbrooke, fixed Hilary with unwelcoming eyes.

'That's because I'm not.'

CHAPTER TWO

*H*ilary's spirits sank. The bear-like gentleman of her earlier acquaintance was none other than the owner of Carisbrooke Abbey! As he stood there glowering at her, she felt herself quail. She had been determined to convince him of her capability and efficiency at their first meeting, and instead she had convinced him of quite the opposite. But there was no use repining; she would just have to go on with what she had been saying.

Fighting down her despondency, she said, as calmly as she could, 'Lord Carisbrooke.' She held out her hand, and endeavoured to control it, for it seemed to have developed an alarming tendency to shake.

He glowered at her for a minute, and then descended the three shallow stone steps that led into the hall.

'There was no one in at the rectory, I suppose. You caught sight of the lights of the abbey through the trees and decided to follow them. Though where the devil the rector can have gone on a night like this—'

'No,' she interrupted him. 'You are mistaken. The rector was in at the rectory, as well as his wife. A charming couple.' She came to a halt, realizing that she was babbling. Taking a deep breath, she continued more slowly, 'They were good enough to lend me their carriage so that I could continue my journey and keep my appointment.' She put on what she hoped was a confident smile. 'I am very pleased to meet you, Lord Carisbrooke. I am Miss Wentworth.'

'I don't give a damn who you— Wentworth?' he asked suspiciously.

'Yes.' She kept the smile fixed to her face.

He regarded her with narrowed eyes and Hilary had to fight an urge to step back as he drew closer.

'Wentworth?' he demanded, his eyes glimmering under beetling brows.

'That's right.' Her smile was now stretched so tight her face was starting to ache. She wanted to lean back, but she fought down the impulse and remained standing upright.

He scowled, and then demanded suddenly, 'Where the devil is your brother?'

She was so surprised she dropped her hand to her side. 'My brother? I don't have a brother.'

'Your father then,' he said dismissively, shrugging himself out of his soaking greatcoat and handing it to Lund. 'He's drunk himself into a stupor, I suppose, and sent you to tell me he's fallen ill and won't be here 'til next week.'

'I don't have a father either.'

His chin jutted forward. 'Then what do you have, Miss Wentworth? An uncle, a grandfather—'

'I have no male relatives, sir – my lord,' she corrected herself.

He looked sour.

Ignoring his expression, she continued, 'I am here in my own right.' She took a deep breath. 'I have come to take up my position as your new librarian.'

'My *what*?' demanded Lord Carisbrooke.

'Your librarian,' she said, though she could not help her voice trailing away a little at the end of the sentence.

'Is this some kind of joke?' he glowered.

'No, I do assure you—'

'Someone in the village put you up to it. A wager, no doubt.'

'Not at all—'

He grimaced. 'Well, you have had your fun. And now you had better leave.'

He prowled over to the door, but before he could open it she spoke. 'It is no wager,' she said.

Something in her tone gave him pause.

'I applied for a position as your librarian,' she went on, taking a deep breath, 'and you offered me the post.'

He eyed her suspiciously, but then seemed to become aware of the young gentleman's interest in the exchange.

'This is none of your business, Ulverstone.'

'But it is so interesting,' returned Mr Ulverstone mildly.

'Harumph! Interesting to you, perhaps, but not to me.' Lord Carisbrooke turned back to Hilary. His chin jutted out. 'I don't know what the devil you're doing here, but it seems I won't be able to get rid of you until I've heard you out. Your claim to be my librarian is preposterous, but I want to know why you're making it, so you had better follow me.'

He turned and strode across the cavernous hall without further ado.

Hilary hesitated.

'I'm most dreadfully sorry,' said Mr Ulverstone, looking at Hilary with an apologetic smile. 'I'm afraid my cousin has never had very agreeable manners, and of late they have become even worse. But if I might give you a word of advice. He is not an easy man to work for. You would be well advised to leave the abbey and seek a position elsewhere.'

Hilary shook her head. Finding an alternative position might seem an easy task to Mr Ulverstone, but before being offered the job at the abbey she had been seeking work for months without success, and Lord Carisbrooke was her last hope. Whatever his manners, she would have to keep the position if she could.

By this time Lord Carisbrooke had almost disappeared. Recalling her thoughts to the matter in hand she hurriedly followed him across the hall, her footsteps echoing on the flags, before venturing into his study. It was of cavernous proportions, but it was at least mellower than the hall. Gold curtains covered the windows and a worn red carpet covered the floor. An oak desk, littered with papers, was pushed to one side of the room. Behind it was a heavy oak chair, carved with spires and pinnacles. In the far corner was a more comfortable-looking chair, set to the left of the fireplace, and standing in front of the fireplace was Lord Carisbrooke.

He was an imposing sight. His large body was encased in buckskin breeches, an ill-fitting tailcoat and a pair of muddy boots. His grizzled hair, covered in raindrops, reached to his collar, and his body was so huge it almost obscured the crackling flames.

His eyes ran over her in one swift, disparaging glance, and Hilary swallowed, suddenly aware of how dishevelled she must look. Her bonnet was battered and her pelisse was soaked. Her hair had come loose of its pins and had escaped her bonnet, straggling in rats' tails across her shoulders. Her face was smeared and her boots were filthy. Her portmanteau was no better, being old and worn.

Still, she raised her chin.

'Now, Miss Wentworth – if you are who you say you are – why have you been trespassing on my property, walking through my woods and then turning up on my doorstep claiming to be my librarian. What do you mean by it?'

She swallowed the qualms that were assailing her and replied, 'It is perfectly simple.' She put her portmanteau down on the floor to give her a minute to steady herself, for he was glaring at her in such a way that her heart was thumping uncomfortably in her chest. 'I answered your advertisement for a librarian, and you wrote back saying that my application had been successful. I have the letter here.'

She took out the crumpled, soggy piece of paper and gave it to him.

He took it roughly out of her hand, eyeing her disbelievingly as he did so. Then he dropped his gaze and read the letter through.

'As I thought, I made you no such offer. This letter is addressed to *Mr* Wentworth.'

Remembering the gleam of admiration she had seen in his eye when she had stood up to him in the woods, she knew that this was a moment when she must be bold, and so she replied audaciously, 'An unfortunate mistake. But not one I hold against you.'

'Oh, isn't it?' The dark pools of his eyes turned to her. They were appraising. 'That is very generous of you.'

But despite his cynicism she could tell that by standing up to him she had not done herself any harm.

'However, I'm not about to offer *Miss* Wentworth a job that was offered to *Mr* Wentworth,' he continued. 'Let this be a lesson to you to tell the truth in the future.'

'I never did anything else,' she replied. 'It is not my fault if you assumed I was a man. I certainly made no such claim.'

'No?' He swept a piece of paper from his desk. 'This is your letter. After telling me of your experience, you sign the letter – but perhaps you had better read it,' he said, holding it out to her.

She looked at the signature, and then met his gaze. 'It says *Hilary Wentworth.*'

'Exactly. Hilary Wentworth. And that isn't you.'

'Yes, it is,' she said, straightening her spine.

'Hilary is a man's name.'

'And also a woman's. I made no mention of my sex in the letter, and you never enquired. I cannot be blamed if your assumption was incorrect.'

'Splitting hairs,' he growled.

'Speaking the truth,' she returned.

He glowered down at her. 'You're very outspoken for a librarian.'

'I have to be. If I don't plead my case, no one else will plead it for me,' she said matter-of-factly.

'Hah!'

She thought she had angered him, but then saw that his face held a grudging esteem.

Suddenly turning the conversation, he rumbled, 'What were you doing in the woods? I gave you directions in my letter. You should have come across the moor. If you had taken my advice you could have cut a mile and a half from your journey, and spared yourself a painful ordeal.'

He glanced at her foot as he spoke.

'I lost my bearings. I went into the wood so that the wind would not whip your letter out of my hands when I read it. As chance would have it, a shower of rain loosed from one of the branches landed on the instructions, smudging the ink. I thought it better to carry on the way I had been going, rather than turn back and face the hill. The rest you know.'

'It's a pity you didn't turn back. There is nothing for you here.'

She flushed, but she was not prepared to give up so easily. Her livelihood depended on it.

Straightening her shoulders, she said, 'I fail to see why not. I can do everything that is required of a librarian. I can arrange and catalogue your library. Moreover, I can work on my own without supervision, something you stated was important to you.'

He regarded her intently.

'You cannot have had many answers to your advertisement,' she continued. 'You appointed me without meeting me, something I am persuaded you would not have done if you had had a choice of applicants. And I am here. I can start work first thing in the morning.'

His bushy eyebrows lifted, and she thought for a moment that her words had swayed him. But then his face closed.

'I can't have a woman in the abbey: it would be sheer stupidity.'

She was startled. What a strange thing to say! Even so, she was not prepared to let the matter rest.

'You will not know I am here. If I work without supervision, then we need never see each other. I will spend my days in the library and I will not get in your way.'

His eyes ran over her assessingly. But then he growled, 'No.'

Her spirits sank, for this time there was a note of finality in his voice.

He pulled the huge, tasselled bell rope that hung next to the fireplace, and a minute later Lund entered the room.

'Miss Wentworth is leaving, Lund,' he said. 'Show her out.'

Hilary was horrified. 'Leaving?'

She glanced towards the rain-lashed windows, and then looked back at Lord Carisbrooke. 'You surely can't expect me to walk back to the village tonight?'

'It would serve you right if I did,' he rumbled. 'But I suppose you will have to stay until the morning.' He turned to the aged servant, who was watching the exchange with a dour expression on his face. 'Lund, take Miss Wentworth upstairs and put her in the Red Room.'

'No good'll come of it,' said Lund with gloomy relish.

Hilary shared his gloom. She was no more desirous of staying than Lord Carisbrooke and Lund were of having her, but she could not venture further tonight.

'Thank you,' she said stiffly.

'There's no need to thank me – as you'll discover. You will leave first thing in the morning.'

It was not a supposition, it was a command.

Cold, wet and tired, Hilary had no more desire to argue. She might be in need of a position, but she had changed her mind about wanting to work at the abbey. She never wanted to speak to this bad-tempered bear of a man again!

*

An hour later, Hilary was finally able to do what she had longed to do all day, and that was to relax in front of a tolerable fire. The time since quitting Lord Carisbrooke's study had not been easy. First had come the painful business of climbing the stairs. Then she had seen why Lord Carisbrooke had told her not to thank him for the use of the Red Room, as it was a cold, cavernous chamber, with its furniture swathed in dust sheets, and an empty grate.

She had managed to persuade Lund to bring her water, logs and candles, and had set about lighting a fire. Then she had pulled the dust sheets from some of the furniture. The first chair she had uncovered had been a heavily carved armchair with a pointed back, which had looked most uncomfortable. Swallowing her disappointment she had uncovered a second chair and had been relieved to see that it was upholstered in faded tapestry. Next she had uncovered a washstand, complete with porcelain bowl; a small table; and finally a four-poster bed. The bed, however, had not been made up. A pull of the bell had eventually brought a grumbling Lund to her room and she had asked him for a pair of sheets. She had been dreading their arrival, fearing to find them dirty or damp, but had been pleased to discover that they were well aired and spotlessly clean. She had made up the bed, then, having seen to the room, she had drawn the heavy damask curtains across the arched windows to shut out the wild night and set about tending her ankle, soaking her shawl in cold water and wrapping it round her foot to reduce the swelling. And now here she was, sitting by a reasonable blaze, with a roof over her head and a bed to sleep in, and for these small comforts she must be thankful.

She examined the shawl. Unwinding it carefully, she was relieved to see that her ankle had almost shrunk back to its usual size. Only the livid bruising showed that she had been injured.

As she lifted her foot gingerly on to a stool she could not help her thoughts returning to Lord Carisbrooke. He was a strange man. A puzzling man. He had an ancient home and a title, and yet he seemed to care for neither. He had grimaced when she had addressed him as 'my lord', and if the Red Room was anything to go by, he neglected his home. He employed, it seemed, only one servant, a man so gloomy anyone else would have dismissed him long ago, and on top of this, he appeared to hate women, for why else would he say he couldn't have a woman in the abbey?

Her imagination took wing. Had he suffered an unhappy love affair in the past? Was that why he buried himself in the abbey? Perhaps. And yet she did not think so, for there had been something tender in the way he had taken her foot and started to unlace her boot.

She shivered slightly as she recalled the way his fingers had brushed against her ankle, touching the skin that had been exposed by her torn stocking. They had been firm yet gentle, the epitome of power held in check, and their touch had set her quivering inside.

It had been a strange feeling, enlivening and disturbing all at once.

Then, too, had been the moment when he had swept her off her feet.

She had been alarmed, and yet she had felt somehow right in his arms. She could still remember the hard ridge of his muscles beneath his clothes, and the way she had trembled at the feel of them.

And then there had been his scent. He had smelled of the wind and rain, of forests and trees, of roots and musk. It had been a masculine smell, with all the strength of nature, virile and powerful.

Her senses had been heightened when she had been near him, she realized. Her body had become finely tuned, reacting to the feel of him, the sound of him, the sight of him, the smell of him. . . .

Discovering that her thoughts were being monopolized by Lord Carisbrooke, she thought it was just as well she was not to work at the abbey. If one afternoon spent in his company could have such a profound effect on her, what would a few weeks do?

If only it was not the one position she had been offered in the last three months. Well, she must just find another position, and find it soon, or she would be destitute.

Perhaps Lord Carisbrooke's cousin would know of something, she thought, brightening. He seemed to be a pleasant young man, and might know of a family who needed a governess. Failing that, perhaps the rector had heard of someone in need of assistance. He and his wife had both been friendly, and they might be prepared to help her. She would call at the rectory on her way back to the village in the morning.

Having settled the matter as much as she could for the time being, she turned her thoughts away from that direction. She did not want to think of the long walk, very possibly in the rain, as the storm showed no signs of abating.

Now that she had settled herself comfortably, she found she was ready for some occupation. She wondered whether she should take *The Mysteries of Udolpho* out of her portmanteau. It was a wonderful book, but perhaps it would be better not to read it in the abbey. Its ghostly apparitions and terrible secrets were spine-tingling enough in a sunny garden; in the cavernous bedchamber they might seem too close for comfort! She decided to take out her needle instead and darn her stocking.

She was just about to begin stitching when a knock came at the door. She gave a start. Really! It was a good thing she had not been reading *Udolpho*, otherwise she would have jumped out of her skin!

Telling herself that there was nothing sinister about the knocking, which would most probably be Lund, come with the supper he had promised her on a tray, she called out, 'Come in.'

It was indeed Lund, but to her surprise he entered the room empty-handed, and said in a surly manner, 'The master sent me to bid you join him for dinner.'

Then, having delivered his graceless message, he departed as gloomily as he had come.

His gracelessness did not disturb Hilary, however. The thought of a hot meal lifted her spirits, and wasting no more than a minute on wondering why Lord Carisbrooke should have invited her to join him, when he had already indicated that he did not want to see her again, she stood up. She wondered briefly whether she should change her gown, but then decided that Lord Carisbrooke would not expect it. Besides, her other two dresses were even shabbier than the one she was wearing. At least her brown linsey-woolsey dress had a high waist, which gave it some pretence to fashion.

She was about to go downstairs when she remembered her hair. Her eyes swept the room. Over in the corner was an item of furniture, swathed in a dust sheet, which could be a dressing-table. She pulled the sheet from it and discovered that she had been right. Her mousy locks were in a dreadful state. Blown about by the wind and drenched by the rain, they were hanging in tangled coils down her back. Unpacking her hairbrush, she loosed her remaining hair, and then brushed it to remove the tangles. Working quickly, she arranged it in a simple knot at the back of her head, then surveyed herself in the mirror with calm grey eyes. She could do nothing about her small, shapeless figure, made even more ungainly by her unfashionable woollen gown, nor could she do anything about her plain features, but she was at least neat and tidy and she was ready to go downstairs.

The descent was difficult. Although her ankle had returned to its normal size, it throbbed every time she stepped on it. She favoured her other foot and supported herself on the banister, until at last she reached the bottom. She hesitated. Then, spotting light spilling out of one of the doorways, she followed it across the stone-flagged hall to the drawing-room.

The leaping fire was a welcome sight. Its logs were ablaze and its flames filled the enormous fireplace, throwing heat into the huge stone-walled room. It was flanked by two heavily carved oak armchairs. Above the fireplace was a looking-glass, set in a heavy frame. A green brocaded sofa was pushed back from the fire, and behind it, on the wall, hung an ancient tapestry. Its colours were faded, but Hilary could just make out the picture of a hunting scene. The carpet was threadbare and the thick curtains were shabby, but they formed an effective barrier across the windows and kept out the draughts.

Sitting in one of the chairs by the fire was Lord Carisbrooke's cousin. And there, standing next to the huge fireplace, was Lord Carisbrooke himself.

The two men made a marked contrast. Mr Ulverstone was fair, with small features, golden hair and blue eyes. He was slightly built, having narrow shoulders and graceful limbs. He held himself well, with an elegance that marked him out as a man of style.

Lord Carisbrooke, on the other hand, was huge and dark. His shoulders were massive and his chest was broad. He made no effort to hold himself well, and leant his elbow against the stone mantelpiece in an attitude of carelessness.

It was not just in terms of physical attributes that the two men made a contrast, but also in terms of dress. Mr Ulverstone had changed for dinner. He was wearing an immaculately cut tailcoat with an embroidered waistcoat, satin knee breeches, white stockings and black pumps, whilst Lord Carisbrooke was still wearing the buckskin breeches and battered tailcoat he had been wearing earlier in the day, and by their poor fit it was obvious they had been designed for comfort rather than show. But despite this, his clothes could not hide the power of his frame. He might look like an unmade bed, but it suited him. He had altogether too large a personality to be confined in the rigid lines of fashionable clothes.

Hilary's gaze moved to his face. It might not be handsome but for all that it had a wild fascination, like the sea on a stormy day, or a vast expanse of rugged moor. There was a compellingness to his features, a stark grandeur that drew her eye and held it.

'Ah. Miss Wentworth.' Mr Ulverstone, rising with alacrity, came forward to claim her attention. 'I am so glad you could join us.'

So this is the source of the invitation, thought Hilary. Mr Ulverstone suggested I should join them for dinner.

'I am sure you are hungry,' Mr Ulverstone continued. 'We will go straight in.'

He offered her his arm.

Hilary hesitated. Somehow it did not seem right that she should be treated as a guest when she was nothing but a librarian, and a rejected librarian at that, but she happened to catch sight of Lord Carisbrooke's frown in the looking-glass and her spirit stirred. She was, after all, entitled to courtesy, and if Lord Carisbrooke was not willing to show it to her, then Mr Ulverstone certainly was. Turning to the charming young man she took his arm and together they went out of the drawing-room.

'What dreadful weather we are having,' said Hilary to Mr Ulverstone.

'Atrocious!' he said, happy to join in with her pleasantry as they crossed the hall. 'I have never seen such rain. I was hoping to return to town today, but the weather would have made it a miserable journey and in the end I decided against it. I can only hope that tomorrow will be better, or else I will have to trespass on my cousin's hospitality for a few days longer.'

Hilary heard a 'Harumph!' behind her, but beyond that Lord Carisbrooke did not comment.

They entered the dining-room. Like the other rooms in the abbey it was large, with walls made of stone. A long table ran down its centre. It would seat about twenty people, and initially Hilary found it overwhelming. But once Lord Carisbrooke had taken his place at the head of the table and Hilary had settled herself opposite Mr Ulverstone, one on either side of Lord Carisbrooke, it did not seem quite so daunting.

Lord Carisbrooke made no effort at conversation, but merely sat looking at her from underneath his jutting brow.

Does he resent me for being at the table? she wondered. Or is he simply taciturn by nature? Whichever it was, she felt she must do what she could to lighten the mood.

'Have you been in the country long?' she asked Mr Ulverstone.

'Almost a week,' Mr Ulverstone replied. 'Ordinarily I live in London. I am a town mouse, rather than a country mouse, I fear! I seldom venture far from the capital, but unfortunately just now it is a sad place to be. I felt I had to get away.' His face darkened. 'The Golden Jubilee celebrations were magnificent, but alas, King George's illness has cast a pall over everything since.'

Lund brought in a large tureen of soup and proceeded to ladle it into three bowls.

'I had heard something of it,' said Hilary, saddened to think of the king's uncertain health, which was causing concern. 'There is talk of it being his old trouble. Do you think it is his madness again?'

At her question Lord Carisbrooke stirred.

Hilary looked at him questioningly. Did he think she would not keep up with the news? she wondered. Did he, perhaps, think she would know nothing of the world beyond gowns and bonnets? Was that why he had refused to appoint her as his librarian, because he wanted someone who was conversant with the topics of the day, and thought that no woman could be? If so, here was a chance for her to show him that she had a lively interest in the world around her, and that she was as well informed as any man.

'It is a great pity,' she went on, knowing from his expression that he was listening to her. 'But the King has been under such a strain recently that it is perhaps not to be wondered at. With Princess Amelia's sad illness and untimely death, he has had much to try him.'

'That is true. He loved Amelia dearly. But the madness became apparent before she died. Indeed, he does not know she has gone, but believes that she is living in Hanover,' said Mr Ulverstone.

Hilary sighed. 'Perhaps it is better that way.'

'I believe you are right,' said Mr Ulverstone sympathetically.

Hilary turned her attention to her soup. She took a spoonful, and found it surprisingly good. She had expected a thin, tepid liquid, but instead it was a good, thick pea soup, tasty, hot and nourishing. After her earlier ordeal in the storm, it was most welcome.

'Is it certain it is his old malady?' asked Hilary, continuing the conversation as she lowered her spoon.

'I'm afraid there is no doubt about it. The symptoms are exactly the same as on previous occasions: the rapid speech, the unnatural excitement, the insomnia and the stomach spasms. I have a number of friends at court, and they are all deeply concerned for the King. His Majesty does not seem to be able to stop talking. It is a terrible outpouring, they say, completely beyond His Majesty's control. He addresses invisible people, and lectures those he knew years ago. It is very distressing for all concerned.'

'Then we must hope he makes a speedy recovery. He always has done in the past. After a few months his symptoms usually disappear, leaving him to resume his life.' She put down her spoon. 'I hope he is being well treated. Some of the things done to him on previous occasions . . .'

'You don't approve?' Lord Carisbrooke broke his silence, and there was an interested light in his eye.

Is he testing me? wondered Hilary, meeting his gaze; is he trying to find out if I have my own ideas? It was a necessary quality if she was to be able to make sense of a neglected library, cataloguing and arranging it without ever disturbing the master of the house. Perhaps he was starting to change his mind about appointing her, she thought. Having considered what she had said about not having a choice, he was perhaps coming to realize that if he did not appoint her he might find himself without any help at all.

Well, she would pass his test.

'No, I don't. I can't see how beating someone can cure their madness, and although I can understand that at times the King might have needed to be restrained, fastening him into a chair and leaving him there seems to me to be barbaric.'

'And yet there are some people who say that that is how we should treat the mad. Lock them away. Tie them up. Beat them into insensibility,' he growled.

'If it was proved to work, then yes, perhaps unwillingly, I would agree. But it doesn't. The poor creatures in Bedlam rarely show any signs of improvement, and if they do, it is despite their treatment, rather than because of it. Besides, the king has always recovered from his malady in the past with or without the help – if it can be called help – of doctors. So of what use were the beatings?'

Lord Carisbrooke's eyes were grim. 'What indeed?'

'What is the word at court?' asked Hilary, turning back to Mr Ulverstone. 'Is it believed he will recover?'

'It is hoped so. But, as usual, it is impossible to be sure.'

'There is talk of a Regency,' said Hilary. 'Prince George is healthy and would be able to rule in his father's stead, until the King recovers.'

'It might come to that. The Prince of Wales would certainly like it to happen. He has been waiting in the wings for long enough. But even if he becomes Regent, will things be any better? There are those who say Prince George is afflicted with the same madness, though in a less severe form. That is perhaps the greatest tragedy, that such an affliction is hereditary.'

'A fine choice of conversation for the dinner-table,' rumbled Lord Carisbrooke. He had been growing increasingly irascible throughout the conversation, and his ill humour had now broken out with full force. 'Miss Wentworth does not wish to talk about such a grim subject, I am sure.'

Hilary almost dropped her spoon in surprise at this sudden concern for her likes and dislikes! Really, Lord Carisbrooke was a most surprising man.

Even more surprising was the fact that Mr Ulverstone seemed unperturbed by his cousin's sudden outburst. In fact, he seemed almost to have been expecting it. 'To be sure,' he replied, 'there are other things to talk about.'

There was a lull in the conversation and they turned their attention to finishing their soup.

Once it was finished, Hilary laid down her spoon and took a deep breath. This was her opportunity ask the question she had been longing to ask all evening.

'You live in London,' she said to Mr Ulverstone, 'and your acquaintance must be large. I was wondering whether you might know of anyone in need of governess, or perhaps a companion?'

'Unfortunately not,' he said ruefully. 'I don't usually hear of such positions – they fall into the province of ladies, you understand. But I will certainly make enquiries as soon as I return to the capital, and if you give me your direction I will write to you as soon as I hear of anything.'

'Thank you. You are very kind.'

'Not at all,' said Mr Ulverstone amiably. 'It is no trouble. You are returning home tomorrow, I take it?'

'I am.'

'Then you must let me take you up in my carriage. You live in Derbyshire, I believe, and it is on my way. My equipage is a comfortable one, and I am persuaded it will make your journey easier than travelling on the stage.'

'That is very kind of you, but I shall not be going home straight away. However, I would value a ride in your carriage as far as the rectory.'

He looked surprised.

'I mean to ask the rector if he knows of any vacant positions in the neighbourhood,' she explained. 'Now that I am here, I might as well see if there are any suitable places.'

For a moment she thought she saw a look of annoyance cross his face, but it was quickly banished and he replied charmingly, 'Of course. Very sensible.'

She must have imagined it, she told herself. There was no reason why Mr Ulverstone should be annoyed at the idea of her seeking employment in the neighbourhood. It was most probably that he was annoyed with his cousin for refusing to employ her, and thereby making her search for an alternative post.

Yes, that was far more likely.

The conversation moved on to general topics, until it was time for Hilary to withdraw. If there had been other ladies present she would have gone with them to the drawing-room whilst the gentlemen sat over their port, but as she was the only lady present it did not seem necessary.

Instead, turning to Lord Carisbrooke, she said, 'I am tired. If I could have a candle, I would like to retire.'

'A good idea.'

He went over to the mantelpiece and lit a single candle from the branched candlestick that stood there, whilst Mr Ulverstone helped himself to a glass of port.

'A word of advice,' growled Lord Carisbrooke to Hilary. 'It would be wise not to leave your room tonight. The corridors have a number of loose flags. You might stumble in the darkness.'

'I am not afraid of a mis-step,' she replied.

'Good. You will need strong nerves if you are to remain here. And not just because of loose flags.' He looked at her narrowly. 'There are some who say the abbey is haunted.'

She felt a frisson of fear before her good sense reasserted itself. 'I don't believe in ghosts.'

'Then you will not be afraid if you hear strange noises, or see an apparition. It is said the abbess walks.'

'The abbess?' she asked, before she could stop herself.

'The abbey is a very old building. The last abbess is said to have cursed my ancestor for buying it, and there are those who claim she has walked its corridors ever since.'

'You are trying to frighten me,' she returned. It was probably another of Lord Carisbrooke's tests. He did not want a woman at the abbey because he thought women were nervous creatures who were constantly having fits of the vapours. Well, she would show him she was not of that sort. She lifted her chin. 'But you will not succeed.'

'It's one thing to be brave in a well-lit dining-room in the early hours of the evening; it is another to be brave, alone in your room late at night,' he said.

He handed her the candle.

As Hilary took it, to her annoyance her hand shook.

By the curve of his mouth, she knew he had seen it.

Steadying her hand, she said repressively, 'Good night, Lord Carisbrooke.'

He gave a grim smile. 'Good night, Miss Wentworth. Sleep well.'

CHAPTER THREE

*T*he wind howled and the rain lashed down. The storm, which had abated during the evening, returned full force in the middle of the night. Hilary slept fitfully and awoke to find herself sitting bolt upright in bed. Her teeth were chattering, her face was covered in cold sweat and she was trembling with the after effects of a bad dream.

The chamber looked ominous in the moonlight. Some of the furniture was still shrouded and under its white dust sheets it looked like misshapen ghosts. Even worse, she thought she could hear pattering footsteps outside her door, the same pattering footsteps that had followed her in her dream. It was only when she had strained her ears for fully five minutes that she was able to convince herself it was no more than the sound of the rain pattering against the window.

Breathing a sigh of relief she lay down again and fell into another fitful slumber, only to be disturbed by an even worse dream. This time she awoke with the conviction that she could hear a pitiful moaning. As she clutched the covers up to her chin she was convinced that she could still hear it . . . until she realized that it was nothing more frightening than the sound of the wind howling in the chimney.

She was just about to lie down again when she suddenly felt the hairs rise on the back of her neck. Once again she was convinced she could hear footsteps in the corridor outside . . . and this time she was not asleep, she was awake.

She froze.

They must be Lund's footsteps as he busied himself about some household task, she told herself bracingly.

But what would Lund be doing out of bed at this time of night?

Of one thing she was certain: if she did not discover the cause of the footsteps, there would be no further sleep for her tonight.

Summoning her courage she threw back the covers and slipped out of bed. She padded over to the fire, and from the glowing embers she lit a candle. Then she crossed to the door and opened it a crack. Peering out, to her astonishment she saw Lord Carisbrooke, dressed in nothing more than shirt and breeches. He was clutching his arm . . . and it was seeping blood. Her common sense immediately drove away her fear. Here was no ghostly visitation, but a man of flesh and blood who needed help.

'What happened?' she asked, hurrying over the cold stone on bare feet.

'Hell's teeth! What are you doing out of bed?' he growled, turning round as he spoke.

His voice lacked its normal strength, and told Hilary more clearly than words that he was suffering from the loss of blood. So ignoring his question, she said, 'Come in.'

She took his good arm and guided him, cursing under his breath, into her room. It was a measure of how much blood he had lost that he went with her.

'Here, sit by the fire,' she said, pushing him into a chair by the glowing embers. Quickly lighting the candles in the candelabra she took a closer looked at his damaged arm, assessing the injury. 'How did it happen?'

'The storm,' he growled through gritted teeth. 'It's blown in part of the attic roof. I heard a crash and went up to see what had happened. There was a gaping hole, and a sudden gust of wind lifted more slates and sent them crashing down on me.'

'They must have been sharp,' said Hilary with a frown, taking his arm and turning it gently between her hands. There was a deep gash in his forearm.

Satisfying herself that it was not beyond her small skill to dress his wound she went over to her portmanteau. She took out a pair of scissors and a number of pins. Returning to him, she deftly slit the fine lawn of his shirt sleeve before gently pulling the fabric away from the cut.

'Where did you learn to do this?' he asked.

His manner was less hostile than usual. Although his voice was a low growl, there was a relenting of his former gruffness.

'My father was a doctor,' she told him.

'And he showed you how to dress wounds?' he asked in surprise.

'I used to go on his rounds with him, and I learned a great deal from watching him. My mother died when I was young,' she explained, 'and my father brought me up alone. He would set me up on his horse in front of him and we would ride together from house to house. Sometimes I would wait in the kitchen whilst he tended his patients, but on other occasions I would be his helper.'

'A strange childhood,' he remarked, but nevertheless he sounded interested.

'In a way. But it was also an interesting one, and it was useful.'

He smiled. 'As you are busy tending my wound, I can hardly disagree.'

'But you would like to,' she said mischievously as she pinned the cut fabric to the elbow of his shirt, so that it would be out of the way when she came to cleaning his arm.

'Hah! Then you think I am argumentative?' he asked with a low growl.

Her mouth quirked. 'I do.'

'And no doubt you think I am bad-tempered?'

She smiled. 'Sometimes, yes, I do.'

'You're a brave woman, Miss Wentworth,' he laughed. 'There are not many people who would dare tell me that to my face, and I would venture to say there are *no* young ladies who would dare. Or who would even want to. Young ladies, in my experience, prefer simpering to telling the truth.'

'I don't believe I know how to simper,' she laughed.

He looked at her appraisingly. 'No, I don't believe you do.'

She went over to the washstand and poured some water into the porcelain bowl. Then she looked around for something to use as a cloth, but she could see nothing suitable. She glanced at his neck tie.

'I need to use something to clean your wound,' she said, going over to him. 'I will have to untie your cravat.'

'Resourceful as well as useful,' he growled, as she knelt down in front of him.

With deft fingers she set about undoing the barrel knot.

'I am,' she said. Then added audaciously, 'Ideal qualities for a librarian who must organize a neglected library without supervision!'

'Hah!' he exclaimed. But by the light in his eye she knew her remark had gone home. 'You don't give up easily. You have experience, I suppose?'

'I do. As I told you in my letter, I helped my uncle to reorganize his library some years ago. I cleaned the books and catalogued them, repairing them as necessary before returning them to the shelves.'

'Your uncle was a gentleman, then?' he asked.

'He was. And so was my father. But whilst my father's interests led him to pursue medicine, my uncle pursued a more usual path. He went to Eton and then to Oxford, where he flourished. He often told me about his years there, and I believe they were the happiest of his life.'

43

'Bandaging wounds, organizing libraries . . . strange occupations for a young lady,' he said, his eyes roving over her face with interest.

'Perhaps,' Hilary conceded. 'But I enjoyed them.'

To begin with she worked at arm's length, but the knot was firmly tied and she had to lean closer in order to loosen it. As she did so she felt his warm breath against her cheek. The sensation was strangely pleasant. It was akin to the sensation she had felt when he had taken her foot, only gentler and yet somehow deeper, setting up reverberations inside her body which she could neither control nor understand. Was it this that made her fingers began to tremble? she wondered. Or were the two circumstances unrelated?

Whatever the truth of the matter, it was making it difficult to untie his cravat.

'Here.' He spoke more gently than usual.

He let go of his arm, and raised his hands to help her. As he did so, his fingers brushed her own.

She gasped. It felt as though she had been struck by lightning.

What had been the meaning of the strange force that had assailed her?

He seemed not to have felt it.

But a moment later she realized he had, because his manner had become gruff again. It was as though the lightning bolt had angered him.

'Let me.' He pushed her hand aside.

Even that slight contact made her shiver inside.

Why was she feeling so strange? Was she ill? she wondered. Had she perhaps taken cold from her soaking? But no, she did not feel ill. Only light-headed, and yet at the same time intensely alive.

He undid the knot and handed her the cravat. As he did so his shirt fell open, revealing a portion of chest. It was broad and powerful, and against her will it drew her eye. Hard ridges of muscle crossed it, covered with dark hair. She felt a sudden urge to reach out and touch it, running her hands across its surface before tangling her fingers in the crisp black waves.

'Your uncle lived near to you, I take it. He must have done, if you helped him with his library.'

His words broke in on her unruly thoughts.

'To answer your question, no, my uncle did not live close to my family. In fact, he lived almost at the other end of the country. But I went to live with him when my father died.'

She went over to the washstand and soaked one end of his cravat in the porcelain bowl. Then she set about cleaning his arm.

'Why did you leave him?'

'He, too, passed away.'

She spoke unemotionally, but in fact it had been a cruel blow.

'He was old,' she went on, 'and he had had a good life. But his death left me with nowhere to go.'

'He did not provide for you?'

'He could not. He had very little. His house was mortgaged, and by the time his debts were paid there was almost nothing left. And so I set about seeking employment.'

She dabbed away the blood. Although the cut was deep, it was now clean.

'You're fortunate,' she said. 'There doesn't seem to be any slate embedded in the wound. It should heal quickly.'

She dried it with the other end of his cravat, then her hands suddenly stilled as she felt his eyes on her.

How she knew he was looking at her she could not have said, for she determinedly kept her eyes on her task. Nevertheless, she knew that he was watching her. She could feel his eyes roaming over her face, tracing the outline of her brow, her nose and her jaw, before coming to rest on her mouth.

She swallowed.

She should not be doing this, she thought suddenly, aware for the first time of the impropriety of the situation. She should not be tending him in her bedchamber, wearing nothing but her nightdress. But it was too late to do anything about it now. She had started, and she must finish the task.

'There.'

Having cleaned his arm, she sat back on her heels, glad to be able to move away from him.

'Thank you.'

His voice was not his usual growl. It was low, but it was husky, and his thanks were genuine.

He was perplexing, she thought, as she stood up. Hard and craggy on the outside, but with something softer on the inside. It called to her, that softness, intriguing her with its hidden depths, and making her wonder what had caused it to be hidden under such a crusty exterior.

But such wonderings were nonsense, she told herself. There was most probably no more to his strange demeanour than an uneven temper. She must not let her imagination run away with her.

He made to rise but, practical once more, she pushed him back into the chair.

'Your arm isn't bandaged,' she said.

She could not use his cravat as it was wet. She looked around the room. The dust sheets were too dirty. There was nothing for it, she would have to use her handkerchief for a pad to place against the wound. It was a pity, for her fine lawn handkerchief was the last good thing she possessed, but it must be done. Then she would have to find something to bind it in place. Her eye alighted on her shawl. It was serviceable rather than beautiful, like all her clothes, but that did not matter for the purpose she had in mind.

First things first. Rising to her feet, she went over to her portmanteau and took out her handkerchief. She folded it into a neat pad and held it over his cleaned wound.

'Here. Hold this,' she ordered him.

'I am usually the one who gives orders in this household,' he said gruffly, but there was a light in his eye that belied his bad-tempered tone.

'Not tonight,' she returned with a smile.

'So I see.'

There was a note of humour in his voice, and he made no further protest. Doing as she had bid him he put his good hand over the pad and held it firmly in place.

Taking up her shawl, Hilary folded it lengthwise and tied it round his forearm.

'There.'

She sat back again and reviewed her handiwork.

'A good job,' he said, looking at it approvingly.

His eyes turned to hers, and she flushed. There was a warmth in his glance that she had not seen there before. It made her feel as though something, hitherto unsuspected inside her, was beginning to unfurl. It was disquieting, and yet at the same time enriching, making her life seem more real. In some strange way she knew that the moment was etching itself on her memory in all its detail. She could not have said how she knew, only that she did: the sight of Lord Carisbrooke, with his grizzled black hair falling in elflocks across his forehead; the glimpse of his chest, with its crisp black hair; the feel of his forearm beneath her hands as she checked his makeshift bandage; the scent of him; the sound of his breathing. And most of all, the aura that surrounded him, of strength, intensity and passion.

The last thought shocked her. But it was undeniable. He was a man driven by passions. By anger, hurt and . . .

He stood up, and the mood was broken.

Hilary shook herself, as though emerging from a dream.

'You had better keep to your room for the rest of the night,' he said, gruff once more. 'The storm is still fierce, and it might dislodge other slates before it is done.'

Hilary nodded.

He went over to the door.

As he did so, the firelight cast strange shadows round him. Some of them made him seem larger, looming and powerful, like the bear she had first taken him to be. But one made a different picture. It portrayed him as a solitary figure. Alone. Haunted.

On reaching the door he turned round.

'Say nothing of this to anyone,' he cautioned her. Adding, 'I would not like to endanger your reputation.'

She nodded.

He opened the door, and then he was gone.

Hilary stood looking at the door for a long time afterwards. His presence had been so strong that she could not really believe that he was no longer there.

Finally rousing herself she tidied away her scissors and pin-cushion, putting them away in her portmanteau. Then, wrapping her arms around herself, she sank into the tapestry-upholstered chair.

She felt exhausted by the events of the last hour. She had done very little, but for some reason she felt as though she had been through an ordeal. Lord Carisbrooke's presence had put a strain on her nerves, not only by causing her to tend his injured arm, but by awakening in her a range of new and turbulent feelings. She was not sure if she liked them. A part of her had found them alarming. They had made her feel as though the ground had suddenly shifted beneath her feet; as though everything she had taken for granted had suddenly tilted, revealing new and hitherto unexpected sides to life. But another part of her had found them wonderful.

Recalling her wandering thoughts she dismissed the feelings. She was tired. That was the problem, she told herself. The strange sensations she had been experiencing had probably been the result of waking in the middle of the night, and then having to dress Lord Carisbrooke's wound. She would feel better once she was back in bed.

Blowing out all but one of the candles she crossed the room and climbed into the handsome four-poster. She snuggled beneath the covers and then blew out the last light.

But try as she might to put all thoughts of Lord Carisbrooke out of her mind, he haunted her thoughts. And when at last she fell asleep he haunted her dreams.

'Come, Caesar.'

Marcus, Lord Carisbrooke called to the large hound the following morning as he crossed the cavernous hall of the abbey. He was dressed for walking out of doors, with a many-caped greatcoat thrown over his coat and his buckskin breeches, and with battered Hessian boots on his feet.

Caesar thumped his tail against the stone flags then rose from his place in front of the fire. He stretched, yawned and padded over to his master, then the two of them went through the abbey door and out of the house.

It was a dismal morning. The sky was grey, threatening more rain.

Marcus turned his steps towards the river. The rain had come down heavily in the night and he feared it would be flooded. If it was, the ford would be impassable.

Why did there have to be such bad weather now, of all times, when there was a woman in the abbey? he asked himself with a frown. And why did it have to be such a disturbing woman? She wasn't beautiful. She wasn't even pretty. She was small and plain. Her eyes were grey, her hair was mousy, and her figure was unremarkable. But still she had unsettled him.

He quickened his pace. His prowl turned into a stride as he crossed the broad, untidy lawns that surrounded the abbey. Beyond them was a gravel path, and further still was a tangled shrubbery where misshapen bushes fought for space.

It was all the fault of that tree! If it hadn't fallen and pinned her by the ankle, then nothing would have happened. But something about the sight of her struggling to free herself had touched him, and cracked the churlish armour that had been gradually growing around him over the last five years. It had been useful, his armour. It had protected him. From pain and hopelessness, fear and foreboding. And ultimately, despair.

All *this* . . . he looked round, his gaze sweeping across the lawns and shrubberies, before glancing over his shoulder to see the abbey itself . . . would soon be gone. With no one to tend it, no new generation to nurture it, it would return to its natural state. The rhododendrons would become tangled, the lawns would become meadows, and the abbey would fall into decay. It was as inevitable as winter following summer; night following day.

It had hurt him to begin with, the knowledge that the abbey would become a ruin, and that the grounds would grow wild. But, bit by bit, he had shut off the overwhelming pain. And now Hilary had made him start to feel again. It should have been unbearable. But for some reason, alongside the pain and despair, was hope.

It was a fool's hope, he told himself harshly. Nothing could change the future. Not even a plain young woman cast adrift in the world and carried to his door.

He tried to turn his thoughts, but they would not be turned. They lingered on Hilary – Miss Wentworth, he told himself irascibly – and his first meeting with her. That tree had much to answer for! Not only had it led to a breach in his armour, but it had led to a reawakening of pleasures he had long since put aside. When he had taken her foot, the feel of it had stirred something inside himself he would have rather left undisturbed.

Oh! but it had felt good.

He gave an unwilling smile. Her foot had been so tiny. And when he had unlaced her boot and his fingers had brushed her skin through the tear in her woollen stocking, her dainty pink ankle had been as soft and smooth as the inside of a rose.

He caught himself up. It was folly to think of such things. Why couldn't she have indulged in floods of tears like any other woman? That would have driven away his feelings. But instead she had reacted to his hostility with pride and stubbornness, rousing his admiration and attracting him more. He had admired her resilience, the more so because he had had need of resilience himself. Different they may be, in gender and wealth and position, but they had something in common: they both knew what it was to endure.

And her resilience was not all he admired. He admired her intelligence, and her tenacity. She had not taken no for an answer when he had declared he would not employ her. He would like to employ her. He would enjoy having her at the abbey . . . .

Bah! Those thoughts were dangerous. The abbey was no place for a woman. For her own safety, she had to leave.

Up ahead he could see the river. As he suspected, it had burst its banks and was now spreading over the adjoining fields. It was muddy and fast-flowing, and swirled in violent eddies as it caught on submerged rocks before continuing on its way.

Caesar was already sniffing at the waters, casting his eyes longingly at a tempting branch that spun just out of reach.

'Come, Caesar,' he growled, as the hound put out a tentative paw.

Caesar hesitated, then bounded back to him.

Marcus surveyed the mass of seething water, hands thrust deep into his greatcoat pockets, then turned his steps towards the ford. It would be under water, but how far under he did not know. Once he had discovered that, he would be able to make a guess at how long the river would take to subside – although even that would be dependent on there being no more rain. He looked at the sky. Grey clouds hung low, covering it completely, and threatening more to come.

He soon reached the ford. The water had covered the grey rock, and was half way up the black, which meant that even without any more rain the ford would not be passable for two to three days, and if it continued to fall, the ford might not be passable for a week. So what was he going to do with Miss Wentworth in the meantime?

She couldn't cross at the footbridge, that was for certain, he thought, as he glanced upriver towards the narrow rustic bridge that spanned the turbulent waters, because beyond it she would be faced with a long walk. He might have been unreasonable enough to suggest that she walk back to the village the night before, but now that his anger had cooled he would not countenance the idea. He could lend her a horse, but his animals were large and spirited, and although she might be able to ride them successfully in the abbey grounds he knew she would not be able to control them over rough terrain. There was nothing for it. She would have to remain at the abbey.

But as soon as the ford was passable again, he would send her on her way.

CHAPTER FOUR

$\mathcal{H}$ ilary woke early. The grey light of morning was drifting in through the arched windows, revealing another gloomy day. It took her a minute or two to remember where she was. The massive stone chamber was so different from her cramped room in the Derbyshire lodging-house that at first she thought she must be still dreaming. But gradually the events of the previous day came back to her. So, too, did her own difficult situation. Lord Carisbrooke had declared he would not employ her, and now she must embark on a search for another position.

She pushed back the covers and climbed out of bed. Going over to the oak washstand, she remembered that she had used the last of the water to clean Lord Carisbrooke's wound the night before. There was nothing for it, she would have to ring the bell and face Lund's surliness. She was just about to do so when she heard a noise on the other side of the door. She jumped; then laughed. It was nothing more sinister than the sound of someone leaving a jug in the corridor! Sure enough, when she opened the door, there was a jug of water. Picking it up, she went back into her room and washed, then set about getting dressed.

She took a dove grey gown out of her portmanteau and put it on. It was, like all her dresses, made of hardwearing linsey-woolsey, and although it was not beautiful at least it was warm. It had a low waist, its bodice buttoned up to her neck, and its sleeves were long. No lace relieved its sober colour. It was plain and unadorned.

Having donned her dress she brushed her mousy hair and arranged it into a knot, securing it with pins before leaving her room.

It was a pity the abbey was so neglected, she reflected, as she walked along the landing, for even in the grey light of the November day she could see that it was beautiful. Its high, arched ceilings were supported by fan vaulting, and its walls were made of golden stone.

She began to descend. She felt like a child, dwarfed by the massive staircase. Its walls were so far apart that she could not have touched them if she had reached out with both hands. The steps, however, were shallow, for which she was thankful. Her ankle was still paining her, and she did not want to put too much strain on it.

At the bottom she hesitated. The hall looked different in the daylight. She could see into every corner of it, as she had not been able to do the day before. She marvelled at the skill of the men who had built it. The huge slabs of stone were perfectly cut, and despite their austerity they were beautiful.

She tried to remember in which direction the dining-room lay. She would not be surprised if she found it empty. If she did, she might have to go without breakfast, for Lund, like his master, did not welcome guests. But when she entered the dining-room she was pleased to see that the table was laid.

The room was warm and comfortable. A huge fire burned in the imposing stone fireplace. The logs crackled, giving off a sweet smell. She went over to the fire and warmed herself.

She had not been there more than a few minutes when Lund entered the room, bearing a tray.

'Breakfast,' he said dourly, taking a pewter platter from the tray and following it with a tankard, putting both on the oak table.

Hilary looked at him in perplexity. The platter contained a hunk of cold beef, and in the tankard was ale.

'For your master?' she enquired.

'His lordship's been up these two hours,' said Lund.

His manner suggested that if she had not been such a sluggard she would have been up two hours herself. Hilary instinctively glanced at the clock, but it showed that she had not been tardy. It was not yet eight o'clock.

Deeming it wiser not to make a reply, she asked, 'Then whose is the breakfast?'

He favoured her with a sour look.

'For Mr Ulverstone?' she enquired.

He gave a heavy sigh, as though he had been tried to the utmost limit of his patience. 'For you. Who else?'

She looked at the meat and ale in astonishment, and then her mouth quirked. The abbey was, indeed, not welcoming to women!

'I will have tea, please,' she said hurriedly, as Lund was about to leave the room.

'Tea?' he asked gloomily.

'Yes, please, tea,' she said firmly. She must have a drink of some sort, and she could not possibly drink the ale. 'You do have tea?' she asked, when he made no move.

'Aye, we do,' he said grudgingly.

'Then I will have a pot, please.'

Still muttering, he left the room.

Hilary sat down and looked at the beef. It was such a large hunk she did not know what to do with it. She was used to having her meat sliced thin, if she had it at all, but this slab would have fed a wolfhound!

Still, she must be grateful she had anything to eat. She picked up her knife and fork . . . and then set them down again as she heard the sound of the heavy front door opening and closing. Footsteps crossed the stone-flagged hall, and Lord Carisbrooke entered the room.

He was looking vigorous. His pallor of the night before had disappeared, and had been replaced by a healthy colour. His large body was encased in his usual badly fitting clothes, but even so she could not help noticing the splendour of his enormous frame. He was a good match for the abbey. Both were magnificent. And both were forbidding.

It was the grizzled hair at his temples that made Lord Carisbrooke seem so, she realized. But beneath the forbidding demeanour she sensed something else, a sorrow deep inside him that his wealth and position could not counteract. She could see it in his eyes. What lay behind his gruff manner? she wondered. And why was he so averse to having a woman at the abbey? Was it because . . . .

But she was becoming fanciful again. Chiding herself for having too much imagination, she bade him a down-to-earth, 'Good morning.'

He returned her greeting gruffly.

Knowing that she might not see him again before she left, she said, 'I will be leaving today, and in case I don't have a chance to speak to you again I would like to thank you for your hospitality.'

'My *hospitality*?' he rumbled, with a lift of his shaggy eyebrows. 'That is a strange word for it!' A spark of humour lit his eye. Then it was extinguished, and something darker took its place. 'As to your leaving the abbey, it's impossible.'

Had he decided to appoint her? she wondered. She felt a mixture of emotions. She would certainly be relieved if she did not have to look for another position, but the atmospheric abbey disturbed her . . . and so did its enigmatic owner.

His next words dispelled her hopes, however.

'The river's flooded,' he said. 'The ford's impassable. You won't be going anywhere.'

This was a blow. Not only was she not to be appointed, but she could not leave the abbey to look for work elsewhere.

'Is there no way across? Surely there is a bridge?'

'There is. But it won't take a coach, and you cannot walk far.'

'Is there no other way out?' she queried.

'None.' He spoke gruffly, and sounded as unwilling to have her as she was to remain.

He threw his gloves on to the table. Then he noticed her platter. 'What's that?'

'Breakfast,' she said.

She could not help it. As she looked at the plate of beef and the tankard of ale, her mouth quirked.

'Breakfast?'

He looked irritated, and then to her surprise he laughed.

It was a rumbling sound and she found it very appealing. It made her think of the sea. It was deep and powerful.

But it was also dangerous.

'I take it this was Lund's idea, not yours?' he asked.

She nodded.

His mood sobered, and she had the feeling that his thoughts had wandered from her breakfast to Lund, and thence down some dark pathway she could not follow.

'What is it?' she asked.

The words were out before she had time to think about them. She had no right to pry into Lord Carisbrooke's private life. But he had looked so haunted that she had wanted to reach out to him.

He looked at her, his eyes gazing into her own, and for a moment she thought he was going to tell her what it was that troubled him. Then the shutters came down. 'You'd better have something else to eat,' he growled.

He crossed to the fireplace and pulled a large bell rope hanging next to it. Somewhere below them, a bell clanged.

Hilary wanted to speak in order to dispel the tense atmosphere that had surrounded them, but Lord Carisbrooke's look was not inviting. He had withdrawn from her, and she dare not venture a remark.

They remained silent. Hilary sat at the large oak table and Lord Carisbrooke stood in front of the massive stone fireplace, until Lund entered the room.

'Some hot rolls for Miss Wentworth,' Lord Carisbrooke growled, 'and chocolate.'

'I've brought her tea,' Lund complained.

'Tea will do very well. I asked for it,' she explained to Lord Carisbrooke.

'Very well. But rolls, Lund, and look sharp about it.'

Having deposited the pot of tea on the table, Lund retreated, grumbling, to fetch some hot rolls.

Hilary's thoughts returned to Lord Carisbrooke's assertion that she would have to remain at the abbey. She had been thinking it over in the long silence, and the more she thought about it, the more she didn't like the idea. Lord Carisbrooke was a man of strange moods, but even so she was drawn to him. Disturbed by her uncontrollable feelings, she felt it would be better if she removed herself from his vicinity.

'How long do you think it will take for the ford to become passable?' she asked him.

He turned to face her. 'Eager to get away?'

Whether he was teasing her, or whether he was annoyed she could not say. She could read neither his tone of voice nor his expression.

'There is no reason for me to stay.'

He regarded her steadily. 'It's impossible to say. It depends on the weather. If it continues to rain you could be here for a week.'

She shivered. The prospect was not inviting.

'If the Red Room isn't good enough for you, you can choose another one,' he growled, with some relenting of his manner.

'Thank you. I think, however, I would rather remain there.' Although the room was cavernous, it had the advantage of being familiar. 'Once I've removed the rest of the dust sheets and opened the windows to let in some fresh air, I think it will be very pleasant.'

He looked disbelieving, but said, 'Very well.'

Lund re-entered the room with a platter of hot rolls. Lord Carisbrooke glanced at them, evidently satisfied.

'You can explore the abbey if you wish to do so,' he said, 'but you are not to venture out into the grounds.'

Hilary was startled by his strange edict.

But before she had time to reply, he said, 'I'll leave you to your breakfast,' and strode out of the room.

Hilary set about removing the rest of the dust sheets from the furniture in her chamber with a will. It was nine o'clock, and after finishing her breakfast she had decided to try and make the room as cosy as possible. She took the large sheets from the furniture carefully, so as not to disturb the dust that had settled on them, and stacked them in the corner of the room. She uncovered another small oak table, which she set on the other side of the bed; a wardrobe; and an elaborately carved settle, which she pulled, with some difficulty, to the foot of the bed. She stood up, straightening her back, and examined her handiwork. The room already looked much better, though it could not be said to appear comfortable. The heavy oak furniture was in the Gothic style with pinnacles and sharp points. The settle in particular looked more like a church pew than a homely seat, and, like the rest of the furniture, had been designed for display rather than comfort. Still, it had an austere beauty about it, and she hoped that when her few personal items were added, the room would have a softer feel.

She arranged her silver comb on the dressing-table, thinking fondly of her mother as she did so, and set her silver-backed hand mirror beside it. Her father had bought them for her mother when her parents had been first married, and on her mother's death they had passed to Hilary. She continued to unpack her portmanteau, taking out her two dresses and shabby petticoat. She was going to hang them in the wardrobe, together with her pelisse, but when she opened it it was musty, and so she arranged her clothes over the back of the settle instead. It only remained for her to put her novel on the table by the bed, and set her half boots by the fire, and she was done. She looked round the room again. It could not be called home-like, but still, it was more welcoming than it had been before she had started her work.

A gleam of sunshine falling through the stained glass window awoke her to the fact that the rain had stopped. The clouds were still low and heavy, but there was a small break where the sun shone through. She was tempted to venture out for a walk. Her ankle was still a little sore, but set against this was her desire for fresh air. If she did not put her weight on her foot, and did not go too far, it should not cause her too much discomfort.

She thought of Lord Carisbrooke's command that she should not venture out into the grounds but decided to ignore it. There could be no reason for it, other than curmudgeonliness, and she had no intention of letting his bad temper deprive her of some exercise.

Taking heart from the break in the weather she put on her pelisse and bonnet then pulled on her gloves. She went downstairs and out into the grounds.

A brisk wind was blowing, sending the clouds scudding across the sky. Despite the present pause in the rain, the bad weather looked set to last. As she followed the gravel path that skirted the abbey, separating it from its wide lawns and untidy shrubberies, she wondered how high the river had risen overnight. She decided to turn her footsteps in that direction. Although she could not see it, she could hear its steady rushing noise, and was in no doubt as to where it lay. She had hardly turned towards it, however, when she saw a young lady coming along the path towards her.

Who . . . ? she thought in surprise, as her eyes ran over the young lady's beautiful face, voluptuous figure, and wonderful clothes. She had not expected to meet anyone on her walk, and certainly not another woman.

Her eyes lingered on the young lady's dress. It was truly exquisite. Made of the finest lace, it looked as though it had come straight out of a fashion plate. Its low-cut bodice was decorated with pink ribbon, and its skirt, falling from a high waist, flowed effortlessly round the young lady's figure before falling in soft folds to the floor. Hilary could not help comparing it to her own dress, which sat lumpishly around her.

So engrossed was she in the details of the beautiful dress that Hilary did not at first find it odd that a fashionable young lady should be wearing evening dress in the middle of the morning. Or that she should be walking out of doors on a cold November day without so much as a pelisse.

'Hello,' she said, with easy, unaffected manners. 'I don't believe I know you. I'm Esmerelda.'

Esmerelda's face was as enchanting as her gown. Her eyes were large and expressive, and her skin was like porcelain. Her nose was short and retrousse, and her mouth was beautifully shaped. Abundant hair was piled in dark coils on top of her head.

'I'm Hilary,' said Hilary. Adding, 'Miss Wentworth.'

'Ah!' said Esmerelda mischievously. 'We are to be formal, then. Very well. I am Miss Varons. How do you do? You are going for a walk, I see. May I go with you?'

'Of course.' The two ladies fell into step. 'I didn't know you lived at the abbey,' said Hilary, wondering whether the enchanting young lady could be a relative of Lund's, a niece, perhaps, or a granddaughter; although the thought of the dour Lund being related to this beautiful creature seemed ridiculous.

'Oh, I don't,' said Esmerelda. 'I'm a guest at the rectory. I have just walked over here. I was tired of being cooped up by the rain.'

'But I thought the roads were flooded,' Hilary protested, before remembering that Lord Carisbrooke had said there was a footbridge.

Esmerelda smiled, then said, 'It has been a pleasure meeting you, Miss Wentworth, but I'm afraid I must leave you now.'

And so saying, she turned and walked back the way she had come.

How strange, thought Hilary. Esmerelda had departed very suddenly. And yet she knew that beautiful young ladies were often capricious, particularly if they were also wealthy. Esmerelda had obviously spent as much time as she meant to on a plain and dowdy librarian.

Dismissing Esmerelda's sudden departure from her mind, she continued on her way towards the river. As she did so, her eyes roamed over the small trees and large bushes that comprised the tangled shrubbery surrounding the abbey.

To her surprise, she noticed something unusual: a pinnacle, rising out of the rhododendrons. What could it be? She hesitated. Curiosity prompted her to investigate, but concern for her ankle, which was starting to ache, prompted caution. In the end, curiosity won. Limping slightly so as to favour her sound foot, she followed a path through the shrubbery, coming at last to a clearing.

In the middle of it was a folly. She had seen pictures of such buildings in her uncle's library. He had been fond of architecture, and had had a great many books on the subject, but she had never seen one in actuality before. It was built in the style of a ruined temple, with tumbledown walls and a gaping roof. Ivy, whether by art or nature, trailed gracefully over the walls. Tall grasses grew between them, and around them grew thorn bushes. But despite the folly's dilapidated state it was elegant and beautiful, its ruination carefully contrived so as to be picturesque.

She was just contemplating a particularly lovely stone, beautifully weathered and covered in moss, when a flock of starlings, startled by a noise, rose into the air. Turning round she saw Lord Carisbrooke.

'Hell's teeth! What are you doing here?' he growled, his brows drawing together forbiddingly. 'Get inside at once.'

Her anger rose. 'I will not be spoken to in such a manner,' she returned. 'And as for going inside, I will do no such thing. I will return to the abbey when I am ready to do so, and not before.'

'It isn't safe out here,' he growled, his eyes flashing with anger.

'Of course it is,' she returned. 'The folly is not going to collapse. It is solidly built and will last for centuries, despite its precarious appearance. There is not the slightest danger.'

'Curse you, woman! Will you do as you're told and get inside?'

'No, I will not! I have every right to take the air, and mean to make the most of it as long as the rain holds off.'

'You will return to the abbey at once, or so help me I'll throw you over my shoulder and carry you there.'

He took a menacing step towards her, but she stood her ground. She could not think what had come over him. He had always been curmudgeonly, but this surpassed anything she had yet seen.

'I cannot believe you mean to lay hands on me—'

But she broke off as he took another step forwards and she saw that he meant to do exactly that.

A sudden thought occurred to her. What if there was danger, and not of the folly collapsing as she had supposed he meant, but of poachers or thieves on the loose?

'If you will give me an explanation of the danger I am in, I will return to the abbey on my own,' she said more softly.

'I cannot,' he growled.

'If I'm in danger, I have a right to know.'

'You are not in danger, as long as you return to the abbey at once.'

'Is it poachers?'

'I cannot tell you any more than I have done,' he rumbled.

It must be something of the sort, she reasoned, to send him into such a taking, although why he would not tell her was beyond her.

However, if there was a chance that there were armed men prowling round the grounds, then she would rather be inside.

She relented. 'Very well, I will go in.'

'I will see that you do.'

He fell into step beside her, his long stride pressing her to go more quickly than she would have liked. Her ankle was hurting, and she was limping badly by the time they reached the door.

'Go in, and don't venture into the grounds again unless I give you leave,' he rumbled, before turning on his heel and leaving her.

Well! she thought, not knowing what to make of the strange encounter. Had there really been any danger, or had Lord Carisbrooke taken leave of his senses? He had certainly been very agitated, but she did not think he would make such a fuss without cause.

Belatedly she thought of Esmerelda. If there were poachers roaming the grounds then Esmerelda, too, would be in danger. But it was too late to do anything about it now. Besides, Esmerelda was probably already halfway back to the rectory.

Sighing deeply, she went indoors. She could not face the long climb up to her room. Nor did she want to go into the drawing-room, where she suspected she would find Mr Ulverstone. At the moment, she did not want company. But she must do something. After a minute's reflection, she decided to look for the library. She was curious to see how large it was, and what kind of books it housed.

Pulling off her gloves, she untied the strings of her bonnet then removed her pelisse and laid it over her arm. She looked about her. Two passages led off from the cavernous hall, one in either direction. One led to the drawing-room, so she decided to follow the other one. She stopped outside the first door leading from it. She hesitated, then went in.

She found herself in what must have originally been the abbey cloisters. Arched windows lined the far wall, making the most of the daylight. It was a very long room, and housed a pianoforte, a sofa and half-a-dozen chairs. Other than that it was bare. There were no tapestries on the walls or rugs on the floor. As well as being a music room, it was probably used for exercise on rainy days, she guessed.

She went out again.

She ignored the next two doors, knowing they would lead into the cloisters further along its length, and instead opened one further along the corridor. It housed a few battered pieces of furniture and smelled musty. She tried the next door, and this time found what she was looking for. She went inside.

The library was an imposing chamber. The ceiling was arched, and the windows were tall and pointed. Huge oak bookshelves lined the centre of the room, and on them was the largest collection of books and manuscripts Hilary had ever seen. They jostled for position, some standing and some lying down, whilst others were stacked in piles with their gleaming spines facing out into the room.

At the side of the room was a pile of dust sheets. They had evidently been removed in preparation for the arrival of the librarian.

She turned her attention back to the shelves. She was fascinated. The library was a treasure trove. She began pulling out some of the scrolls. They dated back hundreds of years. If she had been accepted at the abbey, she would have enjoyed arranging them.

An idea occurred to her. If she made a start on organizing the library then Lord Carisbrooke might change his mind about appointing her. Once he saw that she was diligent, he might decide she could stay. And if not, it would at least give her something to do whilst she was forced to remain.

She laid her pelisse over the back of the chair, and put her bonnet and gloves on the seat. Then she began to empty the first shelf, the one that was easiest to reach. She carried the books, scrolls and manuscripts over to the table and dipped into them to see what they contained. It soon became clear that whilst some of them related to the abbey, being either plans or deeds or other such documents, some were works of learning, and others were works of fiction. The plans arrested her attention. Here was something straight out of the pages of a Gothic romance, for the abbey possessed a number of secret passages. Having seen an age of religious persecution, in common with many old houses it had a number of passages leading to secret rooms where priests could be hidden. Fortunately no such hiding places were needed today.

She turned her attention back to the task in hand. Once she had sorted the ancient tomes she wanted to return them to the shelf. It was, however, very dusty. She went over to the dust sheets. On top of them were laid a number of small rags, evidently intended for cleaning.

She set to with a will, dusting the shelves and then replacing the books and scrolls, now neatly organized. She was just about to start on the second shelf when the door opened and Mr Ulverstone entered.

'So there you are!' he said with a charming smile. He glanced round the room, and evidently realized what she was doing. He frowned. 'I thought my cousin refused to appoint you as his librarian.'

'He did. But I must have something to do, and I thought that if I could make a good job of it . . . .' She trailed away as she saw Mr Ulverstone's expression.

'You must do as you wish, of course, but my cousin does not like to be crossed. I fear he will not be pleased.' His frown cleared. 'But enough of this. Whatever Marcus's thoughts on the matter, you have been working hard and need a rest. I have come to ask you if I can persuade you to give me a game of cards or chess.'

Hilary hesitated. She would really rather continue with her work, but seeing no way out, she gave in with a good grace.

'Willingly,' she said.

He offered her his arm, and together they went into the drawing-room, where the cards had been laid out on an inlaid table.

He held out her chair for her, then sat down opposite her, flicking up the tails of his coat as he did so.

'What would you like to play?' he asked, picking up the cards and shuffling them with a proficient air.

'I don't know many card games,' she confessed.

'Then you should! They form an agreeable way of spending a winter evening. I will teach you.' He put the cards down on the table. 'Would you like to make a small wager, to render the game more interesting?' he asked with a smile.

'I think I'd better not,' she said ruefully. 'I could not afford to lose!'

He laughed. 'You are very wise. In London the stakes are so high that entire fortunes can be won or lost on the turn of a card! Now, I suggest we start with piquet.'

CHAPTER FIVE

*M*arcus prowled back to the folly, looking about him all the while. Once there, he gave it a thorough search and then proceeded to search the shrubbery. At last, frustrated, he turned his steps into the heart of the shrubbery, following what was little more than a track. At the end of it, after several twists and turns, he came to a small cottage. Taking a moment to prepare himself, he knocked three times. The door opened, and an elderly woman opened the door. She was of middling height and had greying hair scraped back from her face in a bun. She was dressed in a black dress with a high neck and long sleeves. On her feet were a pair of stout shoes. Behind her, the cottage looked inviting. Sprigged curtains decorated the windows and cheerful paper covered the walls. The chairs and sofas were soft and appealing. A table pushed to the wall at the left-hand side of the door was covered with a snowy white cloth. And sitting peacefully by the fire with a doll on her lap, was the beautiful Esmerelda.

'Thank God! She's here,' said Marcus as he strode in to the cottage. His words were heartfelt.

The elderly woman shut the door and locked it behind him.

'Yes. She came back of her own accord in the end.'

Having satisfied himself that Esmerelda was safe, Marcus turned to the elderly woman. 'How did she manage to get away, Mrs Lund?'

'I had to go out for some more logs for the fire—'

'I've told you to lock the door behind you whenever you have to leave her,' he growled.

'I did,' returned the elderly woman. 'But she climbed out of the window.'

Marcus looked towards it. It was a very small aperture.

'I didn't know she could get through.'

'Neither did I,' said the elderly woman. 'Until today.'

He breathed a great sigh of relief. 'Well, at least she's back. But we'll have to have the windows barred. We can't risk her getting out again.'

'Lund is already seeing to it.'

He nodded.

Esmerelda, crooning to her doll, had not looked up, but now she turned towards him.

'Hello, Marcus,' she said.

'Hello, my dear.' His voice was gentle. But his eyes were tinged with pain. 'That's a pretty dress,' he remarked, making no mention of her recent adventure.

'Do you think so? Lundy likes it, but I think it's too plain.'

He smiled; but only with his mouth. 'Come, now, Esmerelda, it's made of the finest lace.'

'I know,' she sighed. 'But I do wish I could have silk.'

'I thought you didn't like silk?' he asked, without surprise, as though her capriciousness was well known to him.

'No more I don't. But I like it better than this.'

'Then I will buy you a new gown,' he said gently.

'Will you? Oh, Marcus, you are good to me.' She got up and kissed him.

'But come now, Esmerelda, I want you to do something for me,' he said, taking her over to the comfortable sofa that was set in the middle of the room and sitting down with her. 'I want you to promise me you'll stay in the cottage with Lundy and not venture out of doors, at least until our visitors have gone.'

'You told me it was Ulverstone who was coming,' she said accusingly. Her mouth made a moue of discontent. As she spoke, she looked him in the face. Her eyes were very beautiful, but there was something restless about them. They were like quicksilver, constantly shifting.

'That's right. And you know what Laurence thinks about keeping you here, so it's best if he doesn't see you.'

'I'm not afraid of him,' she said fiercely.

He shuddered. 'No, I know you're not.' Adding silently, It is he who is afraid of you.

'And besides, you lied. It isn't Ulverstone.' Her face became cunning. 'It's a woman.'

He felt his heart contract at the thought that Esmerelda had seen Hilary. When he had found Hilary walking in the grounds he had been horrified, forcing her to return to the abbey in an effort to help her avoid just such an encounter. Fortunately, she had come to no harm.

'I didn't lie,' he said. 'Ulverstone is here, but the young woman is here as well.'

'She isn't very pretty,' said Esmerelda. 'In fact, she's plain.' She smiled, pleased. 'And her clothes are horrible. Did you see her pelisse? It had a patch on the bottom!'

She laughed delightedly.

So that's what saved her, thought Marcus. If she had been well dressed and beautiful . . . His blood churned at the thought of what might have happened. But then he dismissed the feeling. It had not happened. Hilary was safe.

'What is she doing here?' asked Esmerelda.

'She is a traveller, trapped here by the rain. She will be gone as soon as the roads are clear.'

'I think I'll invite her to tea.'

'No,' he said firmly.

Esmerelda grew sulky. 'Why not? She liked me. I know she did.'

'Of course she did,' he said soothingly.

'Then why can't I have her to tea?' she demanded.

'Because I don't want you to.'

She pouted.

'Now, Esmerelda. Do you want a new dress or don't you?' he asked.

'No,' she said vehemently.

'Very well. Then I will not buy you one.' He stood up.

'You will,' she said.

'Only if you do as I ask.'

Her face contorted in to a mask of fury. In a sudden movement she wrenched off her doll's head and threw it at him.

He flinched, but it was not from the impact of the doll's head. It was from love, and pity, and despair.

Her fury abated as quickly as it had arisen. 'You will,' she said again, this time wheedling. 'Won't you, Marcus?'

'As long as you stay in the cottage until our visitors have gone. Then you will have a beautiful gown. Do you promise?'

She looked sulky again.

'Esmerelda?'

'Oh, very well,' she said.

'Good. And now, my dear, I must be going.'

On his way to the door, he said in a low aside to Lund's capable wife, 'Keep a close eye on her. I don't want you to leave her even for a minute until the windows have been barred.'

Mrs Lund nodded. 'Very well.'

Marcus glanced at Esmerelda, then he left the cottage.

Once more in the clean, fresh air, he passed a hand across his brow, then set out to walk off his low humour. Esmerelda was intractable at the best of times, and with visitors in the house she was worse. Her assurance to stay in the cottage did not fool him. She would stay there as long as the thought of the dress held her in check, but once its magic had worn off she would try and escape from Mrs Lund again. For everyone's sake, he would just have to hope she did not manage it.

The rest of the day passed quickly for Hilary. After playing cards with Mr Ulverstone, a game he won easily, they had a light lunch and then she returned to the library. Lord Carisbrooke had not joined them for luncheon but this, said Mr Ulverstone, was usual. His lordship spent his days wandering round his estate, overseeing the tasks that had to be performed in order to keep the abbey in some form of order.

The library soon absorbed her. It was rewarding to sort the books and scrolls, separating fact from fiction, and placing anything concerning the abbey on a separate pile. It was also rewarding to dust and polish the shelves, bringing out the full beauty of the oak.

Towards five o'clock the door opened. Hilary was expecting to see Lund, who had grudgingly promised to bring her tea in the library, but it was not Lund who opened the door, it was Lord Carisbrooke.

He checked on seeing her, then frowned. 'What are you doing in here?'

'Making myself useful,' she returned.

She spoke boldly, but she was not at ease. She did not know what Lord Carisbrooke's reaction would be. He was a perplexing man. His outburst in the grounds had shocked her, and yet strangely it had not frightened her, for she had had the intuitive feeling it masked a real concern for her safety.

'You were not appointed as my librarian,' he growled.

'I must do something to earn my keep,' she said.

He looked at her from beneath beetling brows. 'That will not be necessary.'

'I have never accepted charity,' she said firmly. Now that she had started she had no intention of turning back. 'I don't mean to begin now. If you will not let me work on the library, then you must put me to some other task.'

'Miss Wentworth, you seem incapable of taking "no" for an answer,' he said with exasperation. 'You are without doubt the most infuriating woman I have ever met.'

'I will take that as a compliment,' she said audaciously, knowing she must stand up to him.

'Pah!'

But though he spoke explosively, his eyes lit with a gleam of humour and she knew he was not angry.

'Besides, you cannot find it so extraordinary that I should expect to work for my keep,' she said, encouraged by his expression.

'On the contrary, I find it incomprehensible. I have told you repeatedly that I will not allow you to organize my library. I have invited you to remain here purely as my guest.'

Her eyebrows shot up in astonishment. 'Your *guest*?'

'Despite my atrocious manners, I have invited you to stay until the waters have gone down,' he reminded her, with a quirk at the corner of his mouth.

'I would not describe it as an invitation,' said Hilary, returning his banter.

'Oh? How would you describe it?' Despite his surly tone, a gleam of interest lit his eyes.

'I would describe it more as a curse!' she said mischievously.

'Hah!' He laughed. Then his mood darkened. 'Perhaps you are right.'

She knew at once that his thoughts had turned down some black pathway where she could not follow. She was seized with a sudden longing to tread that pathway with him, to bring him hope and comfort. For all his size and strength, she knew that he was troubled and she was filled with a need to help him. Her hand raised of its own accord. She wanted to stroke his brow, pushing the elflocks back from his forehead, and soothe the troubled expression she saw lingering in his eyes.

She almost did it.

Before reminding herself that to touch him so intimately would be unforgivable.

Her hand fell to her side.

They stood, frozen in time, joined by his nameless sorrow.

At last she managed to recall her mind to the conversation. It might bring him out of his troubles, she thought, to talk about ordinary matters again.

'I must have some occupation,' she said. 'I cannot sit and twiddle my thumbs all day. Give me leave to continue, and make some order out of this chaos.'

To begin with he made no reply. But then, with a visible effort, he roused himself. He pursed his lips. She had the feeling he was about to refuse her again. Then he appeared to change his mind.

'If you must do something, then I suppose it would not do any harm,' he said. 'But you must not feel you need to repay me for your board and lodgings. The service you rendered me last night would be more than sufficient recompense. Which reminds me. I wanted to give you this.'

He pulled her handkerchief out of his pocket. It was white and fresh, and had been newly laundered.

As Hilary took it, she was forcefully reminded of the night before. She remembered every detail of their time together, from the moment she had seen him in the corridor until the moment he had left her room. She remembered the feel of his arm as she had cleaned and bandaged it; the sight of the crisp, dark hairs on his chest; the musky smell of him. And she remembered more. She remembered the rapport there had been between them. It had touched parts of her she had never even known existed, waking in her the desire to help and nurture him. And she remembered the physical tension there had been between them.

It was there again now, that same potent force that had threatened to rob her of her reason. It was threatening to rob her of her reason again. It was making her long to reach out and touch him, and be touched by him.

She made an effort to break the spell.

Thank you.

She tried to say the words but they would not come out. Her mouth was too dry to form them.

She swallowed, and then tried again. This time she had more success. But the words, although they came out, were no more than a whisper.

'You're welcome,' he said.

His reply was bland, but there was an intensity to his voice that made her afraid to look up and meet his gaze.

She busied herself by tucking her handkerchief into the cuff of her long sleeve. But her hand shook as she did so.

'Here.'

He took it from her, and holding her fingers in one of his own large hands, he tucked it into her cuff with the other one. His fingers brushed the sensitive skin on the inside of her wrist and she gasped. The sensation was electric.

His hands stilled.

There was an unnatural silence. It was so intense that Hilary could hear her own heart beating. She knew he was looking down at her, but she dare not lift her gaze. If she once looked him in the eye, she was afraid she would never be able to look away.

Still his hands lingered. One held her tiny fingers in the gentlest embrace, whilst the other remained at her wrist.

The tension was so great that she began to tremble.

He removed his hands, and she began to breathe again, but then he put them on her shoulders. 'You are cold.'

'No.'

'No?' His voice was charged with an emotion she could not understand. It was strong and powerful, a mixture of tenderness, longing and concern, heightened by an electricity that put lightning to shame.

Stepping back, she tried to reclaim her senses. They were confused when he was close by. They could see nothing, hear nothing, feel nothing but him.

And they did not want to.

She searched her mind for some topic of conversation that would break the charge coursing between them.

His injury.

Yes. They had been talking about his injury.

'How is your arm?' she asked.

It was an unexceptionable question, and yet even something as simple as that sent her thoughts spiralling down unwanted pathways. It was all too easy to remember the way it had felt the night before; and to wonder how it would feel if it were to reach out and pull her close . . . .

'Better,' he said. His voice came out in a low, throaty growl. 'It will take some time to heal fully, but I was able to remove the bandage this morning. Your shawl has been laundered, as well as your handkerchief, but I cannot return it to you at the moment. It is not yet dry.'

'And are you able to move your arm freely?' she asked, taking another step back. Even now, he was playing havoc with her senses.

'I am,' he reassured her.

There was less throatiness in his voice, and she gave an inward sigh of relief. Some of the electrical charge was beginning to dissipate, making it easier for her to think.

'You were fortunate,' she said.

She finally risked raising her eyes to his . . . only to see him grimace.

'Fortunate?' he asked.

There was an unusual note of bitterness in his voice, and she had the sudden feeling that there was more to the situation than met the eye. Had he really been injured by falling slates? she wondered. If not, how had he been injured? And why had he lied?

Something tugged at her memory. Some disconnected fact, and yet at the same time connected. Something she had seen in one of the manuscripts she had examined in the library. She tried to capture the elusive memory, but it would not be caught.

She returned her thoughts to their conversation. 'Fortunate it was no worse,' she explained.

His answer were heartfelt. 'That, yes.'

His reply was enigmatic.

She wanted to question him about it but she could see he was lost in his own thoughts. He was looking inwards, not outwards.

Then recalling himself to the present, he looked round the room. 'You've worked hard,' he said. 'And you've made a good start. It's a long time since the library's been so organized. It's beginning to look cared for again.'

He spoke as an employer to his employee. All traces of tenderness and longing were gone. She was glad of it, she told herself. But she could not hide from herself the fact that his tone made her feel hollow.

However, she determined to match his formal manner with a formal manner of her own.

'Thank you,' she replied.

'I cannot keep you at the abbey,' he said, and just for a moment she heard a note of real regret in his voice, 'but I will make sure you have somewhere to go. I offered you employment and you came in good faith—'

She shifted uncomfortably. 'Not exactly. I suspected I had little chance of such employment if I admitted to being a woman, and so I signed myself Hilary Wentworth, instead of Miss Wentworth, deliberately, in order to give myself every opportunity of finding work.'

'That was enterprising,' he said, with a ghost of a smile. 'But still, I offered you work. If things were different . . . .' For a brief moment his eyes lit, and then dimmed again. 'But they are not. I cannot allow you to stay at the abbey, but I will find you some other employment and provide you with lodgings until it begins.'

Then, with a slight inclination of the head, he turned on his heel and walked out of the room.

Hilary walked over to the window. Her calm was destroyed. She did not know quite what to make of Lord Carisbrooke. She was drawn to him, as she had not been drawn to a man before, but there were many aspects of his character she did not understand. Moreover, she did not feel that she would understand him even if she had an opportunity to know him for years, instead of only the few days she was likely to spend with him. There was something secretive about him. And yet she felt it was not because he had a secretive nature, but because he carried some heavy burden. What it could be she did not know. And would probably never find out, she reminded herself. She was becoming too involved; allowing herself to forget that she was only at the abbey because she had been kept there by the weather.

But there was something, all the same, tugging at her memory, that would not let her rest. Something that would shed a light on his injuries; something to do with one of the manuscripts. How it could do so she did not know, but she would know when she found it again.

If only she could remember which one it was . . . .

CHAPTER SIX

*W*ill you take a ride with me? asked Mr Ulverstone a few days later, as he and Hilary finished a game of chess. 'I thought I would go down to the river and see how far the water has fallen.'

Hilary glanced out of the window. The rain had at last stopped. None had fallen that day, and there seemed a real chance that the river would soon return to its normal levels. Mr Ulverstone's offer tempted her. She felt in need of some fresh air. Besides, she was interested to see whether the river was low enough to cross, so that she could learn how much longer she would have to stay at the abbey. She had no riding habit, but that did not deter her: Mr Ulverstone would not expect her to possess such a thing. He had spent a great deal of time with her over the last few days, and she knew that he accepted her status. They had played chess and cards together, and had discussed the topics of the day – because there was little else to amuse him, Hilary supposed. Still it had made a pleasant distraction from her work.

'By all means,' she said.

Not ten minutes later she was in the stable yard behind the abbey, and one of the grooms was helping her to mount a spirited horse. She was apprehensive, for the animal was extremely large. But still, she wanted to visit the river, and she knew that if she needed any help Mr Ulverstone would assist her. Mr Ulverstone mounted a fine bay, and they turned their horses' heads toward the river.

'We will not be kept here for much longer,' said Mr Ulverstone. 'We have had no rain for the last two days, and we should soon be on our way.'

The drive was wet with sodden leaves, but the air was fresh and the ride was enjoyable. The grass to either side of the drive was damp with water droplets which winked as they caught the sun. Further off, the glossy leaves of the rhododendrons shone. Glimmers of colour relieved the green borders, brightening the shrubbery where a few late roses still bloomed. Up above the sky was blue, laced with grey and white clouds.

The horses plodded companionably on their way.

By and by, Hilary heard the sound of rushing water and turning a corner, she saw the river. Even in its swollen state it was picturesque. A rustic footbridge crossed it not far upstream, and willows overhung it. Downstream, it meandered through wide fields, now mercifully no longer under water.

'It doesn't seem too bad,' said Hilary, 'but as I don't know the river . . .'

'This is nothing,' said Mr Ulverstone. 'Another day, and it will have dropped enough to make the ford passable.'

'Then we should be able to travel tomorrow,' said Hilary.

'Yes. I will be glad to get away from the abbey, and return to London. But in one way I will be sorry to leave: I will miss our games. It has been very good of you to play with me. I like nothing better on winter evenings than to settle down by a roaring fire and have a hand of cards, or test my wits at chess.'

'It has been very pleasant,' agreed Hilary. And indeed, without Mr Ulverstone, the time would have passed far more slowly, for she had seen little of Lord Carisbrooke.

'I'm glad you have enjoyed them, too.' His voice was warm. Suddenly he turned towards her and, dropping his reins, reached over and took her hand. 'Miss Wentworth—'

Hilary was surprised. There was something about his tone that made her feel he was about to say something significant. But he stopped suddenly as footsteps intruded on his speech. Looking up, Hilary saw that the rector's wife had appeared on the other side of the river.

Mr Ulverstone dropped Hilary's hand, and a look of vexation crossed his face.

'Mrs Pettifer,' he muttered. He raised his voice so that it would carry across the ford. 'This is a surprise. You have walked from the rectory, I take it, Mrs Pettifer?'

'I have,' said the rector's wife, raising her voice likewise so that they could hear her.

'It is very good of you to have called, but I don't see why . . . ?'

'I've come to see Lord Carisbrooke,' she called. 'My husband's cold has taken a turn for the worse and he's confined to his bed. He won't be able to take the service on Sunday, and as chance would have it the curate's away visiting his grandmother. I don't know what we're to do.'

'One Sunday won't matter, I'm sure,' said Mr Ulverstone. 'The villagers' souls will not be in danger if they miss a week's instruction.'

Mrs Pettifer looked shocked. 'It's not a thing I'd like to see happen. Nor, I'm persuaded, would Lord Carisbrooke. But perhaps he might be able to think of something.'

'Won't you join us?' asked Hilary. 'We are about to return to the abbey.'

'Thank you, I would welcome the company. I will cross higher up, at the footbridge, and join you shortly.'

She disappeared from view, to reappear soon afterwards.

'A good thing it hasn't been swept away,' she said. 'It's been lost before now, when the river was high, but it seems solid enough this time.'

'Would you care to ride?' asked Mr Ulverstone. 'I would gladly take you up before me.'

'Oh, no thank you. As long as you don't go too fast I shall keep up, never fear.'

They set off at a slow pace.

'I'm glad to see you,' said Mrs Pettifer, looking up at Hilary. 'I've some news that might interest you, my dear. The very night you called on us at the rectory, we had a second visitor. A local farmer, Mr Hampson – a very respectable man, and doing well for himself – called to ask my husband to christen his newest daughter. She'd just been born, and wasn't likely to live, and he didn't want her to depart this world without benefit of a christening. So my husband went and baptized the poor child, though he was sneezing fit to burst, and what do you know? She survived the night, and now looks set to live, which is a blessing, because never a better family than the Hampsons drew breath.' She stopped to draw breath herself, then asked, 'Now where was I? Oh, yes, the Hampsons,' she continued, without waiting for a reply. 'And what did my husband say on his return, but Mr Hampson's looking for someone to look after his three little girls until his wife is up and about again.'

The rector's wife looked significantly at Hilary. It seemed she had realized Hilary might be in difficulties at the abbey, and had decided to let her know of Mr Hampson's need.

'That is good news,' said Hilary thoughtfully. 'I'm so pleased the little girl has gathered strength. And I confess, I am interested to hear that Mr Hampson is in need of someone to look after the children, for as chance would have it I am looking for a position myself.'

Although Lord Carisbrooke had promised to find her a position it might take some time, and she did not feel she could neglect this opportunity to do something for herself.

'What a coincidence,' said Mrs Pettifer blithely. 'Now if that isn't good luck all round. Well, seeing as though we've still a fair way to go, let me tell you all about it.'

On their return to the abbey, Mrs Pettifer was soon ensconced with Lord Carisbrooke. Hilary was surprised that he had so readily made time for the rector's wife, but Mrs Pettifer had taken it for granted that he would see her, and Lund had shown her in right away. Whatever his faults, it was clear that Lord Carisbrooke was a responsible landowner who would always make time for his dependants.

It intrigued Hilary. He was short-tempered and she had thought he would be irritated by Mrs Pettifer's visit, but it showed her that, where Lord Carisbrooke was concerned, she had a lot to learn – although she would not have time to learn it.

The thought deflated her. He was the most interesting man she had ever met. Complicated and irascible as he was, he drew her, and she had the strangest sensation that her life would be empty without him.

'Will you join me in the drawing-room and give me my revenge at a game of chess?' asked Mr Ulverstone, as Hilary started to go upstairs.

'Gladly,' she said, turning her thoughts from their gloomy path.

Having repaired to her room to take off her outdoor things and replace her boots with soft shoes, she went into the drawing-room. A large fire was blazing cheerfully in the hearth.

She went over to the side of the room and was about to lay out the chessboard when Mr Ulverstone forestalled her by saying, 'Miss Wentworth, there is something I would very much like to ask you.'

She turned towards him with an enquiring glance.

'I have thought for some time . . . that is, it has not been long, I know, but I feel I know you already. We have had such interesting discussions during our time here, and I have enjoyed our games of cards and chess. Then, too, our occasional rides have been so pleasant . . . in short, Miss Wentworth . . .' Here he went down on one knee. 'Miss Wentworth, I am asking you to be my wife.'

'Your wife?' Hilary was dumbfounded.

He spoke seriously. 'Yes, my wife.'

'But this is all so sudden . . . we hardly know one another . . . and you are from London . . .'

'I have taken you by surprise. I knew it would be the way. I have spoken too soon. Believe me, I would have liked to court you properly, but the circumstances are such that, if I do not speak now, after tomorrow I will probably never see you again.'

'Yes, that is so. But please, you look uncomfortable. Won't you be seated?' she said, flustered.

'Very well. But only if you promise to hear me out.'

Hilary consented. Although it had come as a shock, and although she was tempted to refuse him out of hand, she also knew that she owed him a hearing.

'I can understand your surprise, but please believe me, Miss Wentworth, when I say that my feelings are sincere.'

'We have known each other for such a short space of time, and you must have a large choice of more suitable young ladies amongst your London acquaintance,' she protested.

'It is true that, in terms of rank, I have met many suitable young ladies, but they are shallow and selfish, caring nothing for anything except money and position. I am a man of large fortune, and attract all the worst kinds of attention whilst in town. And if the young ladies are bad enough, their mothers are ten times worse. I have been the target of every matchmaking mama Society has to offer,' he said with a grimace. 'Perhaps now you can begin to see why I have not chosen a bride from amongst the *ton*. I have met any number of beautiful damsels, but I don't care to be married for my fortune.'

Hilary nodded thoughtfully. She had not considered the question from that point of view, but now that he had explained it, his proposal seemed easier to understand.

'Whereas you have shown no regard for fortune or rank. You have spoken to me pleasantly and openly, without coquetry – in exactly the same way as you spoke to Mrs Pettifer, in fact. You see me as a person, Miss Wentworth, and not as a man of fortune or position. I know it is too soon to speak of love, we know each other too little for that, but I have a liking for you, and I believe you have a liking for me.'

Hilary did not reply. A willingness to join him in a hand of cards or a game of chess was one thing; marriage was quite another.

'Unfortunately, I cannot marry you,' she said.

He looked taken aback. But then his features resumed their charming cast.

'Do not give me your answer now. I will not be leaving the abbey until tomorrow. Think it over, I beg you. I am persuaded your life as my wife would be enjoyable. You would have a house in town, and the means to travel. I will not speak of it any further today, it is for you to decide, but I will hope for a more favourable answer to my proposal in the morning.'

The door opened, and Mrs Pettifer entered the room.

'Oh, I'm so glad that is sorted out,' she said, clearly oblivious to what had just passed between Hilary and Mr Ulverstone. 'Lord Carisbrooke is to send for Mr Chibbins – you know Mr Chibbins,' she said to Mr Ulverstone, 'the Reverend Mr Johnson's curate? He doesn't live far off, and can preach the sermon on Sunday. But now, my dear, let me finish telling you all about Mrs Hampson and her daughters.'

Mr Ulverstone, with one last look at Hilary, excused himself as Mrs Pettifer launched into a description of Mrs Hampson.

'Well, my dear, would you like me to tell them you are interested?' she finished.

'Thank you, that would be very kind,' said Hilary.

'Then that's settled. I'll call on them on my way home.'

Mrs Pettifer took her leave, and Hilary repaired to the library: she had neglected her work for long enough.

She set to with a will, taking up where she had left off. As she did so, she thought over Mr Ulverstone's proposal. There was no doubt about it, if she could have brought herself to accept, it would have made her life much easier. Although she was grateful to Mrs Pettifer for telling her of the Hampsons' need, they did not want someone for long, and once Mrs Hampson was up and about again she would be forced to seek another place. Even so, that did not mean she could marry a man she did not love.

For some reason she found her thoughts straying to Lord Carisbrooke. If *he* had . . . but that was ridiculous. Why would an earl propose to a small, plain young woman without a penny to her name?

As if to emphasize the point, she happened to look up and glance out of the window at that moment, and saw Lord Carisbrooke . . . with two elegant ladies. One was young, about twenty-two or three years of age, guessed Hilary, and the other was older, possibly the young lady's mother. They were dressed in the first stare of fashion. The young lady wore a blue riding habit with gold frogging, which set off her dainty figure to perfection. She wore a beaver hat, perched on her golden curls, and carried a whip. The older lady also wore a riding habit. Hers was of a rich purple hue.

How had they come there? wondered Hilary, knowing the ford was still flooded. But then she realized they must have crossed at the footbridge, dismounting and leading their horses across.

'. . . Mama said we couldn't possibly come,' came a silvery voice through the window, 'but I was not going to let a little rain deter me. "We are promised to Lord Carisbrooke for dinner", I said, "and no flooded fords are going to make me break an engagement".'

Her mother laughed. 'Dear Veronica! Always so headstrong! She rules me with an iron hand!'

'Oh, Mama!'

Hilary did not hear Lord Carisbrooke's reply to this badinage. The small group passed out of sight and hearing, evidently going round to the front door. It seemed the two ladies were to stay to dinner.

Hilary glanced down at her shabby gown. It seemed shabbier than ever. She did not relish eating dinner with two such exquisitely attired ladies, and decided it would be better for her to take dinner in her room.

She put aside the books she was cleaning and went out into the hall.

'Ah, Lund. Lord Carisbrooke has guests for dinner,' she said. 'I think it would be better if I took dinner in my room tonight.'

'Guests?' Lund managed to inject a worldful of suspicion into the word.

'Yes, a young lady and her mother.'

'If that bain't the limit,' he grumbled.

But he had time to say no more. The front door opened and Lord Carisbrooke's voice bellowed, 'Lund!'

Hilary slipped upstairs.

For all Lord Carisbrooke's reluctance to have a woman in the abbey, he didn't seem able to keep them out. First Esmerelda, and now the two elegant ladies who had ridden over. But it was evidently not female visitors he objected to – especially such beautiful ones, she thought with a pang – it was females living in the abbey that he would not tolerate.

He would not have to tolerate it much longer, she thought, lifting her chin. She would be leaving shortly. As soon as she had an opportunity to have a word with him in private, she would tell Lord Carisbrooke that she had been offered a position with the Hampsons and let him know that she was ready to depart as soon as they should send for her.

He might not want to offer her lodging until then, of course, for although he had said she could stay until such time as he found her a position, he was unpredictable and might change his mind. But if he turned her out, then she was sure that Mrs Pettifer would offer her a roof over her head until the Hampsons were ready for her.

She wandered over to the window. It was almost dark. The winter evening was already drawing in, and there were stars in the sky. They gleamed and glistened, casting their ethereal light over the ground below. It was a restful scene.

Until something broke the peace. It was a knock at the door. Thinking it must be Lund, she called, 'Come in.'

But when the door opened, it revealed Lord Carisbrooke.

He had changed his clothing, making some small concession to evening. His tailcoat was blue, and was adorned with brass buttons. His breeches were cream, and his shirt was white. But even so, he wore his clothes. They did not wear him.

His expression was bad-tempered. His eyebrows were lowered, and his dark, liquid eyes were pooled beneath them.

'What's all this about taking dinner in your room?' he rumbled.

Ah! So that was it.

'I thought, as you had guests, I would—'

'Skulk up here on your own?' he demanded.

'Relieve you of my presence,' she returned, lifting her chin. She had learnt from experience that she must stand up to Lord Carisbrooke. He was a strong man, and courage was something he respected.

But instead of exploding with a customary Harumph! he asked, 'What makes you think it would be a relief?'

There was something in his voice that told her it was not an idle question. He really wanted to know. Very well, she would tell him.

'The fact that you have done your best to avoid me over the last few days,' she replied calmly. But her calmness was misleading. She had been disappointed to see so little of him, and although her head told her it was a good thing, her heart told her otherwise. 'You have made your feelings about me perfectly clear.'

He looked at her intently, and she felt herself grow hot with the sudden fire she saw in his eyes.

'I certainly hope not,' he said, his voice a low growl.

The words seemed double edged, but she did not dare to ask what he meant. The atmosphere was becoming charged with some potent force that she did not understand and could not control. The air, which a moment ago had been thin, was now thick and heavy, and she was finding it difficult to breathe.

With an effort, she wrenched her eyes away from his and went over to the window. She flung it wide, taking in a deep draught of fresh air. She knew she should continue their conversation, but her heart was beating too rapidly for comfort, and besides, she was being tormented by the memory of him sweeping her off her feet again. His arms had been so powerful, his chest so strong and hard . . . .

Breathing in deeply, she at last mastered her emotion enough to turn the conversation into less dangerous channels. 'Lord Carisbrooke, I have no wish to embarrass you in front of your guests—' she began firmly.

'You seem to forget that *you* are one of my guests.'

'Not in the same way,' she returned. 'They were invited—'

'Miss Palmer has never been invited to Carisbrooke Abbey in her life. She doesn't concern herself over such niceties, and if she wants to come, she invites herself. She is pleased to think that she was engaged to dine here because at our last meeting she said she would wait upon me as soon as her mother recovered from a slight indisposition, and remarked that it would be wonderful to have dinner in the abbey. More than that was never said.'

'Nevertheless, they are—'

'What?'

His eyes were fixed on hers, as if he was challenging her to put the facts into words.

Her heart misgave her. But then she rallied. If he was determined to make her say it, then say it she would. 'Of a different sort. Beautiful, elegant—'

His eyes smouldered. 'Whereas you are not?'

She should agree, but her voice for the moment deserted her.

His eyes never once left hers. 'No – thank God. You are stubborn and headstrong, and completely uncontrollable, but beautiful and elegant you're not.'

She felt a twist of pain. It was one thing to know it herself, it was quite another to have it spoken of . . . and spoken of by Marcus. As he stood there looking at her, his hands clenched by his sides and his eyes burning with some unnamed emotion, she was over-whelmed by a sudden desire to be the most beautiful creature he had ever seen, a breathtaking vision with golden ringlets and ivory skin, cornflower eyes and rosebud lips; an alluring damsel clothed in the finest silks and the most expensive laces, who would make him fall at her feet.

But this was folly! She would never be such a vision.

Her plainness had never troubled her before, but now it was a cause of great regret. She was, and always would be, a little, plain woman, shabbily dressed.

But there was no use repining. So she fought down her unhappiness and said, 'Then I can't see why you would want me to join you.'

He looked at her long and hard.

As the silence grew she shifted uncomfortably. His eyes seemed to see more than other people's. They seemed to see not only what was on the outside of her, but what was on the inside.

'Oh, can't you?' he said at last. 'Then you can't see very much. Curse it, Hilary . . .'

He stepped towards her, and her heart stood still.

She could tell that he wanted to touch her. For all that she was little and plain, she knew that he wanted to caress her.

And she wanted him to.

He stopped.

By the way his hands were clenching and unclenching at his side she could tell that he was at war with himself. Would he step forward and touch her? Or would he fight the impulse, and remain where he was?

The atmosphere was full of expectancy.

And then she saw his expression change, and some of the tension ebbed away.

'Well, never mind,' he said, as though with a great effort. 'I want you there, and that is enough.'

Struggling to master her emotion, she said, 'I beg your pardon, but it is not enough. I am not at your beck and call. I am accustomed to making my own decisions.'

'So I've noticed.' There was a touch of wry humour in his voice.

Against her better judgement she smiled, too. 'Then you will realize my mind is made up.'

He regarded her steadily. 'I see that it is. Very well, then. What if I *ask* you?'

'I beg your pardon?' She could not believe she had heard him correctly.

'If I *invite* you to join me for dinner, instead of commanding you?'

She was nonplussed. 'I suppose . . .' Her mouth quirked despite herself. She doubted if this man had ever asked anyone for anything before, and she meant to make the most of it. 'I suppose I will not know until it happens!'

'Hah!' His eyes smouldered with enjoyment at her mischievousness. 'Very well, Miss Wentworth.' He made her a low bow. 'Will you do me the honour of joining me for dinner?'

She could not resist. 'The honour is all mine,' she said, dropping him a mock curtsy. 'I accept.'

His mouth spread into a broad smile.

Not all the smiles in the world could make him handsome, but Hilary would have rather looked on his face than on the beauty of an Adonis. It had character and humour, depth and strength. Ugly though it was, it was fast becoming her model of perfection.

'Then I will see you at eight o'clock,' he rumbled.

CHAPTER SEVEN

$\mathcal{H}$ ilary hummed to herself as she went about making her toilette. There was nothing she could do about her shabby clothes, but she took down her hair and brushed it a hundred times, until it shone. Then she arranged it in a more elaborate knot than usual, securing it with her mother's comb, a hair decoration she kept for special occasions. She teased out a few small curls round her face and then she was done. A glance in the mirror showed her that her eyes were sparkling, and she had the satisfaction of knowing that, although plain, she was in her best looks.

A moment later she reproved herself for her vanity. Just because Lord Carisbrooke had invited her to join him at dinner did not mean that . . . She cut off her thoughts, before they could wander down dangerous paths. His invitation was no more than kindness. Indeed, it was no more than common courtesy, and if she read anything else into it, then she was a fool.

It was a good thing she had sobered herself, for as she went downstairs Miss Palmer's silvery laugh greeted her before she had even entered the drawing-room. She had never heard such an enchanting sound.

'Oh! Lord Carisbrooke! You must not say such things,' Miss Palmer was protesting.

Quite what Lord Carisbrooke had been saying Hilary did not

know, but by the sardonic look on his face it did not appear to have been amusing. Miss Palmer seemed pleased, however.

'Why not?' asked Mr Ulverstone charmingly. 'Your habit does indeed match your eyes, my dear Miss Palmer. It cannot catch their sparkle, however. That could only be caught by sapphires.'

Miss Palmer gave another silvery laugh. 'How you all flatter me!' Then, hearing the door open, she turned her exquisite head towards Hilary. Her golden ringlets danced, and her rosebud mouth formed a surprised 'o'.

She was, thought Hilary, the most exquisite creature in creation. She looked like a fairy, so fragile and dainty was she, and her dress accentuated the impression. She had changed out of her riding-habit – evidently she and her mother had brought a pack horse with them – and was wearing an ethereal gown of spangled gauze. Its puffed sleeves were decorated with knots of blue ribbon and its soft fabric draped itself appetizingly round her slender curves. In the candle-light, the spangling shimmered and shone. Around her throat was a simple necklet, drawing attention to the whiteness and beauty of her skin, and satin slippers, peeping out from beneath her gown, revealed tiny feet.

Beside her, Hilary felt like a gargoyle.

Her spirits fell, and she wished she had not made a fool of herself by trying to do something a little more becoming with her hair. The few curls she had tried to tease out around her face were nothing but a mockery when compared with Miss Palmer's ravishing curls. To make matters worse, she could see a satirical look in Miss Palmer's eye.

'Well, well, what have we here?' enquired Miss Palmer.

Her voice was musical, but her words had a cruel edge.

Hilary felt her stomach contract, but a moment later she straightened her spine. Miss Palmer's beauty had temporarily overawed her, but this was no fairy, no matter how like one she looked. This was a young woman, and, Hilary was beginning to suspect, a spiteful one.

Miss Palmer looked Hilary up and down, and a contemptuous smile broke out around her mouth.

'Do tell me,' she said, turning to Lord Carisbrooke, 'who is this?' She managed to invest the word *this* with a world of disdain.

'This is Miss Wentworth,' said Lord Carisbrooke, looking at Hilary with a warm light in his eye. 'She has been helping me to reorganize the library.'

Miss Palmer's beautiful eyebrows raised an inch. 'How very peculiar. But still, she is dressed for the part. Where *did* you get that dress?' she asked Hilary. 'What an ugly thing it is. Mama, did you ever see such a thing? It looks more like a sack than a gown. But its colour is admirable. It is so dull already, it will never show the dirt!'

She dissolved into silvery laughter.

'No, indeed,' replied Hilary, refusing to be cowed. 'The dress is most practical.'

Miss Palmer went into further peals of laughter. 'Imagine wearing a dress because it is practical! I would as soon ride a horse because it has four legs!'

'Oh, Veronica,' laughed her mother, dabbing at her eyes with an embroidered handkerchief, 'you are too droll!' She turned to Lord Carisbrooke. 'Isn't she, my lord? Veronica has always had the readiest wit!'

'Indeed,' said Lord Carisbrooke. 'Miss Palmer is most amusing.'

Clearly missing the acid note in his voice and taking his words at face value, Mrs Palmer said, 'And so she is, my lord. Everyone agrees. Why only last week dear Toby was saying that Veronica makes him laugh more than anyone he has ever met in his life!'

'Mama,' said Miss Palmer, blushing beautifully. 'Lord Carisbrooke doesn't want to hear about Toby Grinston, even though he is a duke!'

'And a fine catch,' said Mrs Palmer, watching Marcus for his reaction. 'But Veronica will have none of him, for all his fifty thousand a year.'

'Mama!' said Miss Palmer, in the most delightfully outraged tones. 'You must not say such things.'

'Then let us talk of something else,' said Marcus.

Miss Palmer looked put out.

Mrs Palmer, covering the awkward silence that sprang up, said bad-naturedly to Hilary, 'Well, girl, don't just stand there. Don't you have some work to do?'

'I have finished for the day,' Hilary replied calmly.

The Palmers might be doing everything in their power to belittle her, but she was not going to answer in kind.

'Well, you must have remarkably little to do,' said Miss Palmer spitefully, having recovered from her reverse. 'When servants work for Mama, she makes sure they earn their pay. Don't you, Mama?'

'Yes, my angel, indeed I do. Servants who are not kept fully occupied are apt to get above themselves.' She turned to Lord Carisbrooke. 'Having someone to organize your library is no doubt a good thing, my lord, the abbey being such a venerable old building that it would be a shame to neglect it, but you must not allow your servants to take advantage of you. If you had a wife, of course, it could not happen. Women know how to manage these things. They take care of servants and relieve you from all the day-to-day trouble of running a home. You should think about taking one, my lord. The abbey needs a mistress. A well-bred young lady who would be able to manage your household and make sure your servants knew their place.'

'It is kind of you to take such an interest in my domestic concerns,' remarked Marcus drily.

'It is no trouble, I do assure you. As your neighbour I feel it is my duty to give you a little hint now and again. But enough of this talk about servants,' said Mrs Palmer, dismissing Hilary from the conversation, even if she did not have the authority to dismiss her from the room. 'Tell me, Lord Carisbrooke, are you going to the Grants' ball next week?'

'Oh, yes, Lord Carisbrooke, do tell,' said Miss Palmer, who was clearly growing tired of having no part in the conversation, and was now all smiles again. 'We are so hoping to see you there, are we not, Mama?'

'We are indeed, my angel.' She turned to Marcus. 'And who knows, my lord, at such a fashionable gathering, you might yet meet a wife?'

Miss Palmer and her mama continued their determined assault on Marcus, flattering and teasing him. He did not appear to enjoy their attentions, but neither did he discourage them.

And why should he? Hilary asked herself. Seeing him with Miss Palmer came as a timely reminder that the young beauty was the kind of woman he was likely to marry. He might not like her, but she was of his world, and would be a suitable match. Perhaps, even now, he was formulating a plan to make her his wife.

A part of her thought that such an idea did not fit with what she knew of his personality – he clearly had no liking for Miss Palmer, and Hilary could not imagine him marrying without it – but another part of her said that she must not let her thoughts degenerate into wishful thinking. If he married a young lady he did not much care for, simply because she was eligible, he would be doing nothing more than leading the life led by most other man of his rank; a lifestyle that held no place for a penniless, plain young woman.

Her spirits sank.

But that was irrational. Why should they?

Only because Lord Carisbrooke was the most intriguing man she had ever met. He was rude, it was true, and yet beneath his gruff exterior lay something very real. What it was she did not know, but she wanted to find out. What drove him? What troubles had shaped his character? Why was he so curmudgeonly? And why had he let her see something softer that lurked beneath?

Mr Ulverstone addressed a remark to her, and she gave him her attention. She must not let her preoccupation with Lord Carisbrooke show.

It was not long before Lund came in and announced dinner. Lord Carisbrooke gave Miss Palmer his arm, which she took with alacrity, fluttering her long eyelashes at him and favouring him with one of her sweetest smiles.

Mr Ulverstone hesitated. Hilary could see that he was torn. He should, by rights, offer his arm to Mrs Palmer, but clearly he did not want to do so. Besides, having offered his hand to Hilary, he no doubt felt he should offer her his arm as well. Mrs Palmer settled the matter for him by taking his arm without waiting for it to be offered, and almost dragging him into the dining-room, leaving Hilary to follow on behind.

The time spent over dinner was no better than the time beforehand. Miss Palmer continued to simper and flirt, and her mother indulged her, whilst Lord Carisbrooke did nothing to check her. If Hilary could have excused herself, she would have done so. The conversation ranged over people and topics she knew nothing about, and no attempt was made to include her, so that she was glad when dinner finally came to an end.

The ladies rose.

Once in the drawing-room, the full extent of Miss Palmer's spiteful nature was revealed.

'You needn't think to set your cap at Marcus,' she said, as soon as the drawing-room door was closed behind them. 'He is not so lost to all sense as to marry you.'

'I never thought he was for an instant,' returned Hilary, stung.

'Oh, didn't you, though? Your kind are all the same. Scheming, nasty little hussies, on the hunt for a rich husband so that you can force yourselves on your betters. But you have no need to put on airs with me. I know what you are, don't I, Mama?' she asked, appealing to her mother for support.

'Of course you do, my angel. But you have nothing to fear from this drab creature. Lord Carisbrooke is not such a fool that he would pay her any attention when there is someone so much more beautiful nearby. Pray, do not distress yourself, my cherub. Now, what are you going to wear at the Grants' ball?'

Miss Palmer became voluble on the subject of her dress, saying to her mother, 'The white satin, I think, Mama. Or perhaps the embroidered muslin. Which do you think will be most likely to bring him up to scratch?'

Disgusted by the Palmers' conversation, Hilary slipped over to the door.

'Aye, about time too,' said Miss Palmer, as she reached it. 'Sitting in here, aping your betters. Get back to the servants' hall, where you belong.'

Hilary left the room with a feeling of profound relief.

Once outside, she considered what to do. It was still too early for her to retire, and so she decided to repair to the library, where she could continue her work until it was time for bed. She had almost finished organizing the first bookcase before dinner, and she wanted to see how it would look when it was done.

She crossed the cavernous hall and went into the library. The fire was still burning in the grate, but the candles were not lit. By the light of the fire she went over to the mantelpiece, and took a candle from the candelabra. Bending down, she lit it at the fire's small flames, then used it to light the other candles. They shook and shivered before blossoming into life.

She turned her attention to the bookcase. It now presented an ordered appearance. Although it would most probably have to be rearranged when the other bookcases were organized, for the time being it was almost done. Everything pertaining to the abbey was arranged on the top two shelves, scrolls and manuscripts on the top shelf and books beneath. Then came the works of learning. Previous

Carisbrookes had been interested in natural history and science, and books on travel were also well represented. Underneath came the novels.

She turned her attention to the table. A pile of books lay there, waiting to be sorted. Once she had done them she would have completed the first bookcase. Carrying a many-branched candlestick over to the side of the room, and placing it carefully so that no wax could spill on to any of the books by accident, she continued with her work. She had not been working for more than a quarter of an hour, however, when the door opened, and to her surprise, Lord Carisbrooke appeared.

'What are you doing in here?' he growled. He stood in the doorway, and the candlelight did not reach as far as his face. It was shadowed, and she could not read his expression.

'I had some work I wanted to finish,' she said.

'Did you indeed?' He came in. The door swung to behind him. 'You should be in the drawing-room, entertaining my other guests.'

'I don't think I like their idea of entertainment.'

'Do you not? You surprise me. Two hours ago, you were telling me that you were not fit to share the same table with them. I see your feelings have changed.'

She made no reply.

'Can it be that you wanted to get away from the estimable Miss Palmer? Or perhaps it is her mother who does not suit your taste. Tell me, Miss Wentworth, which of my guests does not take your fancy?'

'I really don't think it is for me to say.'

'But I am asking you, and I require a reply.'

Still she said nothing.

'I shall, and will, have one,' he said.

'Very well,' said Hilary, turning to face him, 'as you have asked, I like neither of your guests.'

'And yet you were singing their praises earlier in the day. Elegant, I believe you described them as, and beautiful. Do you find Miss Palmer lacking in elegance, now you have seen her close to?'

'No, I do not,' she answered him honestly.

'Then it is her beauty that is lacking.'

'No indeed. She is everything that is lovely.'

'She is, is she not? Those golden curls . . . that rosebud mouth . . . . She is like a fairy, wouldn't you say? Tiny and ethereal, with a face and figure that are both enchanting.'

Hilary's spirits sank, but she could not help agreeing.

'And yet you do not like her.'

'No, I don't.'

He pursed his lips. 'Do you know why she comes here?' he asked.

'No.' She busied herself with the books, hoping he would leave her. The conversation was proving decidedly uncomfortable.

'Because she wants to be the next Lady Carisbrooke,' he said. Hilary's hands stilled. She had suspected as much. But to hear the words from his own lips made her grow cold.

'You don't approve,' he said.

There was a strange note in his voice, part mocking, part hopeful, part questioning.

With an effort she roused herself from the deadness that had gripped her and began to sort the books again. 'It isn't for me to approve or disapprove. Your choice of wife is your own concern. I would not presume to offer an opinion.'

'Then you think I should marry her.'

It came out as a remark and not a question.

She stopped what she was doing. She should say nothing. It was not her place. And besides, she could not trust herself to speak rationally on the subject. But something inside her would not be denied. She turned to look at him. Then, folding her hands in front of her, she said, 'No, I do not.'

'Oho.' A gleam of something unfathomable lit his eye. 'You don't think I should marry her. Why not?'

There was no turning back. She had started. She must continue.

'Because she will not make you happy,' she said. 'She is selfish and shallow, and she will not help to heal your pain.' Her spirit spoke to his. 'She will not dispel the darkness inside you.'

There was a deathly hush.

In the silence she became aware of every inch of him. She saw the hurt in his eyes and the droop of his mouth, the fall of his shoulders and the clenching of his hands.

He stood there like a statue, before her, and she became aware that he was fighting an inner battle. She dared not move. She dared not breathe. If she did, she was afraid of breaking the moment and pushing him back into his private hell.

The logs crackled in the hearth.

Then even they became still.

But it was not peaceful. There was no true contentment. Instead, the silence was ominous, like the calm before a thunderstorm.

I should not have spoken, she thought with sudden fear, as the tension began to mount. The air was becoming thick, buffeting her with a force that emanated from him as he wrestled with his inner demons. It grew and grew, until it had become almost unbearable in its intensity.

And then it broke in great tidal waves, and the crusty armour with which he had surrounded himself began to crack. She could see it happening as he stood there in the candlelight. His whole body began to change. The tension that had twisted him was cracking and splitting asunder, and beneath it he was coming to life. The pain was on the surface now, where she could reach it, and heal it . . . if he would let her.

'Do you think a wife could do that?' he asked.

Her eyes were drawn to his and she felt herself grow weak.

But now was not the moment for weakness. Now was the moment for strength.

Lifting her chin, she said, 'I do.'

She saw him walking towards her, and she began to tremble. Every inch of her began to shake. She longed for him. For his touch. His caress.

And then he was standing in front of her.

She could feel the heat of him, generated by his body, as it almost touched hers. She could see the lines on his face. They were etched across his forehead. She could smell the musky scent of him. She could see the rise and fall of his powerful chest, and feel the whisper of his breath on her skin.

'Perhaps there is one who could manage it,' he said throatily.

Then the air was filled with a new energy, a freshness and vibrancy that made her spirits soar. Her focus sharpened. She saw him with greater clarity than she had ever seen him before; she noticed every hair, every pore, every bristle on his chin.

As he lifted his hand a shiver ran over her from the top of her head to the soles of her feet. Every one of her senses was heightened, and without him even touching her he made her body react.

She could tell by the look in his eyes that the experience was as new to him as it was to her. It was unexplored territory for both of them, this powerful attraction of body, spirit and soul.

As his fingers stroked her face, her shivers intensified. She felt as though no one had ever touched her before.

'So smooth,' he said, as he ran his fingers over her skin. 'So soft,' he said, as he turned his hand over and trailed the back of it across her cheek.

She trembled with anticipation.

'Your skin is like the petal of a rose,' he murmured huskily. 'When I brushed your ankle through the tear in your stocking on the day of our first meeting I was aware of it, and I have never forgotten the feeling. I have dreamed of it ever since.'

He ran his fingers over her head. They were impeded by her knot of hair. He pulled out the pins, and let it fall about her shoulders. Then he ran his hands through it.

'You should not be doing this,' she protested.

But she made no move to stop him. It felt wonderful to be cherished by him. She cared nothing for the danger, but wanted it to go on for ever.

'I know.' He took her face between his hands, and looked deeply into her eyes. 'Better than you can ever do. But for one sweet moment I want to pretend . . .'

His voice tailed away. He bent his head. He kissed her. As his lips brushed hers she trembled from head to foot. The touch of his lips was so gentle that she barely felt it, but she felt its effects as it sent rivers of tingles up her arms and down her legs. She was drowning in the new and wonderful feelings, enlivening, exhilarating, almost unbearable in their intensity. And then, as his mouth moved more firmly over hers, it took her to another world altogether, opening up new horizons she had never even dreamed of. She found herself responding, her mouth moving under his with instinctive understanding, and a passion to match his own.

His arms slid round her waist, pulling her closer, and in return her arms twined themselves round his neck.

They were so close there was nothing between them. The line of their bodies met and held, the front of his jacket merging with the wool of her gown, so that it was impossible to tell where he ended and she began.

She felt him deepen the kiss and her lips parted in unknowing invitation as he traced the line of her lips with his tongue. She was lost to all reason, forgetting that she was a lowly librarian whilst he was an earl; forgetting, too, that a secret still lay between them; knowing only that it felt wonderful to be held by him and that she never wanted the moment to end.

She had never known it would feel like this to be kissed. It was an explosion of senses, an exhilaration she had never even dreamed of, an all-consuming experience that almost overwhelmed her. She revelled in the feel of his mouth, the texture of his lips, the taste of him, a sensation so new yet so right she felt she had been born to experience it. She was locked in the moment, no future, no past, only present, with Marcus pressing her closer and devouring her with his kiss.

There was a slight noise, but she did not want to hear it. She didn't want anything to pierce her haze of bliss.

But Marcus had heard it, too.

He pulled away from her, and she knew he had been recalled to reality by the slight sound.

Hilary tried to restore her breathing to its normal levels, then glanced towards the door.

The sound had been an unmistakable click, as though the door had opened, or closed. To her relief, there was no one there. If they had been discovered in such a compromising position . . . but they had not.

Could it have been the wind? she wondered. If a stray gust had rattled the door, could that perhaps account for the sound they had heard?

'We had better return to the drawing-room,' said Marcus. 'We have been away too long.'

Her heart sank. The openness that had existed between them for a few short minutes had gone, and he had buried his demons deep again. She knew he would not tell her what was tormenting him.

She could only hope that the moment would come again. But for now it had disappeared.

Gathering her thoughts, she said, 'That isn't a good idea. I have already left it once. I have no reason to return.'

'Perhaps you are right. It won't do to tempt the Palmers' spite. I will go alone.'

She watched him leave the room, then sank down into an enormous oak chair. What had been the meaning of his behaviour? Why had he kissed her? And what had been the meaning of her own?

She gazed into the fire, as though it might hold the answers.

She had told him he should not be kissing her, and he had said, 'I know. Better than you could ever do'. His words had been enigmatic. She had not noticed at the time – she had not been in a condition to notice – but now she wondered about them. Was it because she was in his house, and therefore under his protection, that he felt he should not have been kissing her? Or because he knew that he had no intention of marrying her? Or had there been some other reason for his strange words?

Whatever the case, she knew beyond a shadow of a doubt that she could never marry Mr Ulverstone now. It was not because she thought Lord Carisbrooke would marry her. On the contrary, she was certain he would not. Even so, she could not regret their kiss. It had been the most breathtaking experience of her life. She could still feel its after effects reverberating through her entire body. Not only were her lips tingling, but her limbs were trembling. It had been the most intimate sensation she had ever experienced, and the most exhilarating. She would not have missed it for all the world. But having experienced it, she knew she could never marry another man. It would be impossible.

By and by, she turned her attention back to the library. She still had some work to do before she went to bed.

Slowly she roused herself. She stood up, pinning her hair back into a knot, and went over to the table once more. She had a dozen or so books still to arrange.

She let her gaze wander over them. They would not take her long to do. Then slowly and methodically, she began to work. Arranging the books was soothing. Gradually, it had a calming influence on her spirit, and the tremors that had coursed through her body began to dissipate. She was relieved. They had been making it difficult for her to concentrate on her task, but at last they disappeared altogether.

She unrolled the next manuscript to see where it should be shelved . . . and then stopped. This was the manuscript she had seen before, the one that had been tugging at her memory.

Her eyes travelled over it rapidly. It contained a plan of the abbey, and was a more detailed version of one she had glimpsed on the previous day. It showed the floor plans, and they revealed something that made her apprehensive: there was only one staircase to the attic on her floor, and it was to the west of her room. She felt herself grow cold. When Lord Carisbrooke had passed her door, seeping blood, on her first night in the abbey, he could not have been not been coming from the attic as he had claimed.

She felt a shiver of apprehension. If he had not been coming from the attic on the night he had been injured, then where had he been coming from?

And why had he lied?

Suddenly, the abbey seemed a darker place.

She had allowed herself to grow close to its enigmatic owner, but what did she really know about him?

No, she would not doubt Marcus. She trusted him. Perhaps the plans were not accurate. They were very old.

Even so, she knew she could not let the matter rest until she had discovered the truth of the matter for herself.

In a fit of rashness, she almost took a candle and made her exploration at once, but her common sense reasserted itself and she knew she must wait until morning. Then she could explore at her leisure, and in the clear light of day.

CHAPTER EIGHT

*C*an *I keep her?*

That was the thought that plagued Marcus as he paced his room later that night. The abbey had turned him from a man into a surly beast, but in a few short days Hilary had breached his defences and turned the beast back into a man.

And how had she done it, this plain little woman? By seeing through his irascibility to his tortured soul beneath.

He thought of what she had said to him in the library: 'She will not dispel the darkness inside you.'

It had cut through the last of his defences. She had known he had dark places, and known they needed illuminating, and she had been right. Miss Palmer could never do that. But Hilary could. He knew it with certainty. She could pour the light of her understanding into the blackest corners of his mind, easing his burden and brightening chasms so deep and dark he had thought they would never see the light of day.

But could he let her? Had he that right? No. A thousand times no. If he decreased his burden, he would surely increase hers. He would dim her life, not all at once, but gradually, as she came to understand the secret that haunted the abbey, and to learn that there was no escape.

He was under no illusions about her feelings for him. Though he had known her for such a short space of time there was a deep and intuitive bond between them, and she was already halfway to being in love with him. But he could not let it go any further, though he longed to with all his heart. She had come into his life and shown him what it was to be human again, and if she was half in love with him, then he was at least half in love with her.

Which was why he must send her away.

The thought made him grow cold. She was the break of sun through the clouds, the first breath of spring, the rain after a drought. But he could not let her love him. He had to let her go. She was young. She would forget him. The passage of time would do much to alleviate her feelings, and with occupation and enjoyment, it would be accomplished. Already he had written to a friend of his late mother's who lived in Bath, and who would offer Hilary a position as a companion at his asking. Her duties would be light, and her company congenial. There would be time and opportunity for her to visit the libraries, to enjoy the Assemblies, and to experience Bath's other pleasant distractions. Then, too, her salary would be generous, and would provide her with the comforts and small luxuries she now lacked. Some pretty clothes, a collection of books . . . And in time she would meet someone else. Bath had a large number of visitors and she would have an opportunity to get to know a variety of people, at last marrying and enjoying the life she deserved. She would marry a learned gentleman, perhaps, or some other good man who would give her an establishment, with the added blessing of children.

He ground his teeth at the thought of her in the arms, and the heart, of another man, but it had to be. He might want to give her all the things she lacked, providing her with a home and a family, but he could not – not without taking her to the mouth of hell and forcing her to look into its gaping maw.

If only he could keep her . . .

But he could not. As soon as the roads were passable he would send out his letter, and within a very short space of time he hoped to have Hilary settled in a comfortable and rewarding life.

What did it matter if the thought of it made him grow cold? In time he would not be sensible of it. In time, he would be sensible of nothing at all . . . .

Hilary slept badly. She rose with the first light, and having washed and dressed quickly she slipped out of her room. She turned left and continued along the landing in the direction from which Lord Carisbrooke had been coming on the night he had been injured. The landing was hung with tapestries on her left-hand side, and on her right there was a banister protecting her from the drop to the hall. The first tapestry showed a battle scene, and Hilary found herself wondering whether it had been stitched by Lord Carisbrooke's ancestors. If so, it must have taken the Carisbrooke women years to complete. The men and horses were strangely flat and oddly shaped, but the stitches were beautiful. Next to the tapestry was a mirror, then came another tapestry.

Then the landing turned a corner, whereupon the tapestries continued on her left whilst a row of windows were now on her right. So far Hilary had come across neither staircases nor doors. From where had Lord Carisbrooke been coming when he had been injured? she wondered.

She went on. Another tapestry adorned the wall, portraying a hunting scene. A man on horseback was winding a horn, and hounds were running free. But still there were neither staircases nor doors.

Up ahead of her the corridor came to an end. She went right up to the wall. It rose before her in all its golden beauty, as solid as a rock. She was nonplussed. Lord Carisbrooke had definitely been coming from this direction, but what could he have been doing in an empty corridor? And how could he have been injured? she wondered, looking up to see if there were any holes in the roof. She saw none.

She turned and began to walk back down the corridor, feeling perplexed. But just as she was passing the tapestry of the hunting scene it billowed outwards, as though there was someone standing behind it. How could they have got there without her seeing them? she thought, as icy fingers clutched at her chest. Her heart began to beat more rapidly. What if the abbey *was* haunted?

Common sense told her it was impossible, but there was definitely someone coming out from behind the tapestry. Someone dressed all in black.

Hilary gave a sigh of relief as the figure emerged. It was not a ghost but a human being of flesh and blood; an elderly woman with gaunt features, and iron-grey hair scraped back into a severe bun.

They stood face to face, looking at each other in surprise. Then the elderly woman's face quickly set itself into a conventional expression. 'Can I help you, miss?' she asked, breaking the silence.

'I . . .' Hilary was at a loss for words.

'The stairs are that way,' said the elderly woman firmly.

'Th-thank you,' stammered Hilary.

Feeling foolish, she turned and walked back along the corridor. But her morning's exploration, instead of satisfying her curiosity, had only roused it more. Instead of reading a Gothic romance, she seemed to have found herself embedded in one. What dark secret hung over the abbey? And how was the mysterious woman in black linked to it? Her sudden appearance had been remarkable. How had she materialized behind the tapestry? Who was she? And what was she doing in the abbey?

Hilary was still wrestling with these problems when, fifteen minutes later, she sat in the dining-room sipping her breakfast cup of tea. The woman had either been hiding there, for which Hilary could see no reason, or she had emerged from a secret door, hidden behind the tapestry. Or perhaps not even a secret door, Hilary told herself, knowing that she must not let her imagination run away with her. Perhaps it was an ordinary door which was hidden by the tapestry for the simple reason that the tapestry was too large to hang elsewhere.

With the tea and rolls inside her, in the full light of day, this seemed the most likely explanation.

It left a number of other questions unanswered, however. Who could the woman be? And why was she in the abbey?

Perhaps she could ask Mrs Pettifer for information, thought Hilary, as she saw that kindly lady coming down the drive. Mrs Pettifer would know all about the household, and would perhaps help her to solve the puzzle.

Before long, Lund had shown Mrs Pettifer into the drawing-room and Hilary had joined her, sitting opposite her by the roaring fire.

'The Hampsons are so pleased to know you will help them in their hour of need,' said Mrs Pettifer, settling back comfortably into her armchair. 'It is not easy to get anyone in this remote part of the world, particularly with your refinement. If you have decided to accept the position, they would like you to start tomorrow.'

Hilary was downcast. She should be grateful that the Hampsons wanted her to start so soon, but she did not want to leave. Her attraction to Lord Carisbrooke might be dangerous, but it was also compelling, and her heart sank at the thought of never seeing him again.

Then, too, if she was forced to leave the abbey at such short notice, what would become of her desire to discover its secret?

And yet she could not turn down this opportunity of employment. Her situation was too precarious to allow her any choice.

She fought down her feelings and replied calmly, 'Yes, I have decided.'

Mrs Pettifer beamed. 'Good. I am so pleased. It must have been difficult for you here,' she said comfortably. 'Lord Carisbrooke's a difficult man, and he doesn't like to have women about the place.'

Hilary was at once alert. Here was just the opening she needed to ask about the strange woman in black, and she was determined to make the most of it.

'Why is that?' she asked.

Mrs Pettifer looked suddenly conscious, as though she had said too much.

'Oh, I expect it's just a foible,' she said hurriedly. 'You know how these great men are. They all have their little ways.'

'The abbey is not completely without women, however,' remarked Hilary.

Mrs Pettifer looked anxious.

'It has been nice for me to find that I am not the only female here,' Hilary pressed.

'You mean . . . you have seen another one?' asked Mrs Pettifer hesitantly.

'I have. An elderly lady. Dressed in black.'

Mrs Pettifer seemed relieved.

'Ah. Mrs Lund,' she said.

Mrs Lund. So that was who the woman was. Hilary nodded thoughtfully. It made sense.

'What is she doing here?' A thought occurred to her. 'Is she the housekeeper?'

There was a barely noticeable hesitation on Mrs Pettifer's part, before she said, 'Yes, that's right.'

So. The mystery was solved.

Hilary chided herself for having been so fanciful. She had been imagining . . . well, really, she did not know what she had been imagining. But she had learnt her lesson. She would not indulge in such foolishness again. The mysterious woman was nothing more sinister than Lund's wife, who looked after the abbey.

'Well then,' said Mrs Pettifer, rising, 'I'll tell the Hampsons you'll be with them tomorrow, and they'll send the trap for you. The waters have gone down, and the ford is passable again.'

'Thank you for your efforts on my behalf,' said Hilary, standing, too.

'I was only too glad to help. I shouldn't like a daughter of mine . . . yes, well, you'll be safely with the Hampsons tomorrow, and never a better family drew breath.'

'And please, give my best wishes to Esmerelda,' said Hilary.

Mrs Pettifer looked dumbfounded.

'Your guest,' said Hilary. 'I met her when she walked over to the abbey.'

'Is that what she said?' asked Mrs Pettifer.

Hilary was startled by Mrs Pettifer's strange reply, but being determined not to become fanciful again she told herself that it could easily be explained if perhaps Esmerelda had not been invited. The beautiful young lady might have invited herself. In that way she would be a guest and yet not a guest. She was a distant relative, most probably, who had paid a surprise visit, and was, therefore, not entirely welcome.

'Well, never mind. Don't see me out, my dear, it's cold in the hall, despite the fire,' went on Mrs Pettifer, becoming bustling again.

She left the room without giving Hilary a chance to say anything more.

When she had gone, Hilary's thoughts turned to the library. She should continue to sort the books, achieving as much as she could in the short time left to her, but somehow she could not bring herself to do it.

What had really happened to Lord Carisbrooke on the night his arm had been wounded? she wondered. Had he been hurt by falling tiles, as he had claimed. Or had his injuries had another cause? Why had he been coming from the direction of the hidden room? What could he have been doing there?

Perhaps it was the housekeeper's room, she reflected. Perhaps he had made his way there when he had been injured, intending to ask for Mrs Lund's help and, not finding her there, had stumbled back along the corridor, where he had been discovered by Hilary.

She gave a sigh. She had only theories. She knew nothing for sure. But if she went up to the attic she would discover one thing, at least. She would see if there really was a hole in the roof, as he had claimed.

Having taken her decision, she went upstairs. She passed her bedroom then followed the corridor until she came to another staircase, the foot of which she had glimpsed from the door of her room. It led upwards, to the roof.

It was much smaller than the staircase that led from the hall to the first floor. Instead of being wide with shallow steps, it was spiral. The treads were worn at the front, where countless feet had passed. She would have to be careful if she was not to slip.

Lifting the hem of her dress, she began the ascent. Halfway up there was a narrow window to her left, showing the abbey grounds spread out in all their autumn glory, but she did not stop. She was uncomfortable on the confined staircase and hurried upwards. At last she came to the top. She found herself in a corridor with two doors leading from it, one to the left, and one ahead. Dropping her skirt, she went into the room to her left. As soon as she entered it, she knew it had been a schoolroom. There were six wooden desks arranged in two rows. Momentarily distracted from her quest, she went over to them. Two of them were carved with initials – LC on one, and RC on the other. The LC was small and discreet, hidden away at the side of the desk. Hilary imagined a little boy sitting there, whiling away a boring lesson by setting his mark on his desk, whilst at the same time making sure it would avoid his schoolmaster's notice. RC, on the other hand, had carved bold, scrawling initials across the top of the desk. There had been no desire to hide his handiwork. A naughty child, or an arrogant one, she guessed. Perhaps his master had told him off, and he had been chastened; or perhaps he had replied, 'I am soon to be Lord Carisbrooke. I can do as I please.'

A master's desk stood at the front of the room. It was covered with maps, a pointer and a globe. They had been left in position, and were it not for the fact that they were thickly coated with dust, Hilary could have believed that the schoolmaster – or mistress – was just about to return.

She recalled her thoughts to the task in hand. Looking up at the ceiling, she ascertained that there was no hole.

She left the schoolroom and went into the second room. It had evidently been the servants' quarters. There were six iron bedsteads, two of which still had their mattresses, although these were now mildewed, a battered cupboard, an empty fireplace, and a chamber pot.

As she made her way through the room she examined the roof, but she could see no signs of storm damage. It seemed that Lord Carisbrooke had lied. But why?

She was about to go downstairs again when she noticed a small door leading out on to the roof. Perhaps the damage was outside? If the door had been blown open on the night of the storm, then the slates could have fallen through.

Now she was here, she was determined to check every possibility. She opened the door, which was set into the sloping ceiling. Picking up her skirts, she climbed out on to the roof.

A bracing wind hit her. She steadied herself against it. Then, standing up fully, she swept her glance over the roof. At first sight she could see nothing amiss. No missing tiles. No holes.

She glanced over to the parapet. She would have a better view of the surrounding roof from there. Having no fear of heights, she walked across to the edge. She was protected by the parapet from a fall. She turned and looked back at the roof, but again she could see no sign of storm damage. Then how had Lord Carisbrooke been injured?

Abandoning the perplexing thought for the moment she turned and looked out over the surrounding countryside, drinking in the view. It was magnificent. From her high vantage point she could see for miles. The English landscape, spread out before her in all its autumn glory, was beautiful. The clouds had given way to blue skies, and the sun, whilst possessing no strength to warm her, made the countryside gleam. The russet colours of the deciduous trees, brown, orange and yellow, were set against the emerald grass and glowed like jewels.

Her eyes roved to the west. Here she could see the rectory, and the crossroads where she had lost her way. She could see, too, the woodland in which she had taken shelter and first met Lord Carisbrooke.

She let her eyes linger on the other houses she saw nearby, wondering which one belonged to the Hampsons. Was it that one, set in a clearing? Or was it the larger house set halfway up the side of the surrounding moor? She let her eyes rove closer to the abbey. She could see the folly, and she could see the roof of another building, by the look of it a small cottage. A gardener's cottage, no doubt, set amongst—

Bang!

She jumped. What was that? She looked round. The door to the attic had slammed shut.

Oh! She laughed with the release of tension. A gust of wind must have caught it! But the bang had given her quite a fright.

She looked once more over the countryside, enjoying the magnificent scene. Then, having not found what she was looking for, she decided to go back in. She returned to the door and pulled it . . . but it remained firmly closed. She pulled again, harder this time, but still it did not move. She frowned. It had opened easily on her way up. She felt her heart begin to beat more quickly. She was on the roof, and no one knew she was there. If the door would not open . . . but of course it would open. It had simply blown shut, that was all. She took a minute to steady her pulse and then tried again. But still it would not move. Not even an inch. If she had not known better she would have thought that it was locked. But who could have locked it? And who *would* have done, whilst she was outside?

Anyone who did not know she *was* outside, she realized.

She began to beat on the door with her fists. If someone had indeed locked it, then she must let them know immediately that she was outside, before they went downstairs again, beyond the sound of her voice. 'Help! Open the door! I'm on the roof!' she called.

But there was no reply.

She tried again, louder this time.

But again there was no reply.

She fought down her rising panic. It was true that she was trapped on the roof, and that she had no pelisse or bonnet, and that the wind was cold, but someone must soon realize that she was missing – at lunchtime if not before – and then they would come looking for her. True, it would take them some time to find her on the roof, but sooner or later someone would remember they had closed the door and would realize she must have been outside.

She did not want to wait that long, however. Clouds were blowing up, and the wind was growing colder. She decided she would just have to attract attention to herself. It should not be too difficult. Lord Carisbrooke usually went for a walk in the morning, and Mr Ulverstone often went for a ride. If she looked out for them, then as soon as she saw them in the grounds below she would wave and shout and attract their attention. Then they would release her.

There was also the possibility of someone hearing her from inside.

She resolved to beat on the door at intervals, and call, so that if anyone was passing the attic stairs they would hear her and come to her aid.

Having decided on a plan, she felt better. She wrapped her arms around her for warmth, being glad, for the first time in her life, that her dress was made of linsey-woolsey, and not of muslin or gauze. In a flimsy dress she would be ice-cold in minutes, but in her service-able woollen gown she would be able to keep reasonably warm.

She went over to the parapet and looked down. There was no sign of anyone in the grounds below at present, but she stayed there for some ten minutes before returning to the door, trying it again in case it was simply stuck, rather than locked. After finding it no more will-ing to move than before she banged on it and again called for help, telling herself that if Mrs Lund was going about her housekeeping duties on the first floor she would undoubtedly hear.

But it was to no avail.

Never mind. She did not despair. The view was very pleasant and to keep up her spirits she decided she would occupy herself with seeing how many buildings she could see. Then, when she was rescued, she would look them up on a map of the area and in that way begin to learn something about the neighbourhood in which she would be living.

She had hardly begun when, looking down, she saw Mr Ulverstone passing across the yard on horseback. She called out. The wind was blowing towards him and she had every hope it would carry her words. For a moment she thought it had done. He turned his head and she waved and jumped in order to attract his attention . . . but then he turned his horse's head and she realized he must not have seen her after all.

Never mind, she told herself.

Even so, her spirits were low. No matter how much she told herself that she would soon be discovered she was beginning to be seriously ill at ease. It was cold on the roof. The sky had clouded over and it had started to rain.

Enough of this, she chided herself. Though the wind was cold and the drizzle unpleasant, the worst that could happen to her was that she would take a chill.

She looked around for shelter, but seeing none she crouched down behind the parapet in an effort to get out of the wet. It was no good. She stood up again, walking beside the parapet to stimulate her circulation and keep herself warm.

To begin with it worked, but gradually the cold seeped into her. It started with her skin, and began to work its way through to the bone. How late was it? she wondered. Was it lunchtime yet? Had she been missed? Or had her absence gone unnoticed? If Lord Carisbrooke was absent for lunch, as he often was, and Mr Ulverstone assumed she was with his cousin, then she might not be missed until dinnertime. And by then she would be a block of ice. She was just wondering whether she should attempt to climb over the roof and see if there were any other doors leading inside when she heard a noise in the attic below. There was someone there!

She scrambled over to the door, forcing her numbed limbs to move.

'I'm here!' Her teeth were chattering, and her voice came out in a thin wail. She tried again. 'I'm here!'

'Hilary!' It was Lord Carisbrooke's voice.

Her spirits rose. He had heard her!

The door opened. Caught off her guard, she tumbled through it . . . straight into his arms.

He growled with relief as he caught her. Then his relief turned to anger. 'Curse it, woman! What are you doing on the roof?'

His words were sharp, but the tenderness of his voice was unmistakable.

'I . . .' Her voice tailed away. What could she say?

He held her against him more tightly. His warmth was wonderful. It was like a glowing fire to her, so cold was she.

'You're freezing,' he said. 'Put your arms round my neck.'

Her numbed limbs had difficulty in obeying, but she managed to do as he said. She could feel his warmth seeping into her as he held her close.

Then, going out into the corridor, he carried her to the head of the spiral stair. With sure feet he was soon down. Turning right, instead of left, he took her into a large chamber. With a shock she realized it was his bedchamber. The four-poster bed was ancient. Crimson curtains were hung around it, made of a heavy damask which were perfect for keeping out the abbey's draughts. A red coverlet matched the curtains. On the floor beside the bed was a faded rug. A shaving table stood in the corner. There was a wing chair, an ornate fireplace, and a fire blazing in the hearth.

'I must go back to my room . . .' she said, as he set her down. She turned towards the door.

'It's not warm enough. The fire has gone out.'

'How do you know?' she asked in surprise.

'Because it was the first place I looked for you when I couldn't find you.'

She hesitated.

'Here,' he said, unstoppering a decanter by the bed and pouring her a glass of brandy.

'I can't—'

'Drink it. It will warm you from the inside,' he explained.

Hilary took the glass. Her hands were still trembling with cold, but she managed to set it to her lips. She took a sip . . . and felt her eyes water.

'You surely don't drink this for pleasure?' she coughed.

'Sometimes. If I can't sleep. Are you feeling any better?'

'A little.' The brandy was starting to do its work, and the warmth of the room was reviving her.

'Good.' He took the empty glass from her. 'Take a seat,' he said, indicating the chair by the fire.

Reluctantly, she sank into the wing chair. If the fire had indeed gone out in her room, which was all too likely, it would be folly to return before she had warmed through.

'Now tell me,' he said, leaning against the stone mantelpiece, not three paces away from her, 'what were you doing on the roof?'

She gave an inward sigh. She did not want to tell him, but she found she could not lie to him.

'I wanted to see if there were really any slates missing.'

His brow darkened.

'I saw the plans for the abbey when I was organizing the library, and I realized that you could not have been up to the attics when you were injured,' she explained. 'You were heading towards them, and not away from them.'

He pushed himself away from the mantelpiece. 'I knew I shouldn't have let you near the library. You are too intelligent for your own good. And so you went up to the attic to see for yourself?'

'I did.'

'And then?'

'When I couldn't see any storm damage I was about to go back downstairs, but then I noticed the trap door. Suspecting that it led on to the roof I opened it. I climbed out, meaning to see if there was any damage noticeable from outside, but then the door slammed shut.'

He grunted and settled back into his former position.

'I tried to open it, but I discovered it was locked. Either Lund or Mrs Lund must have come into the attic and, seeing it open, shut and locked it without realizing anyone was outside.'

He looked at her from beneath lowered brows.

'Mrs Lund?' he asked darkly.

'Yes.' It was clear he had not wanted her to see the housekeeper, although why that should be she did not know. 'I saw her this morning. I was exploring, wanting to see where you had been coming from on the night you were injured, and as I walked along the corridor she came out of the room behind the tapestry.'

He threw up his hands in disgust. 'It's impossible to curb your curiosity.'

Hilary smiled, but then the smile became rueful. 'They say that curiosity almost killed the cat, but when I climbed out on to the roof, I'm lucky it didn't kill me. If you hadn't found me when you did . . . .'

'Luck had nothing to do with it,' he said, his charcoal eyes smouldering. 'I was looking for you.'

She glanced at the clock, thinking that in that case it must be later than she had expected, only to see it was not yet twelve o'clock. She raised her eyebrows questioningly.

'I had a particular reason for wanting to find you. I wanted to speak to you about my cousin.'

'Mr Ulverstone?' she asked in surprise.

'The very same. Mr Ulverstone, I understand, has asked you to marry him.'

'How do you know that?' she asked in amazement.

'I know everything that goes on in the abbey. I forbid you to accept him,' he said.

'You *forbid* me . . . ?' asked Hilary.

'I do.' His tone was unrepentant. 'It is not the tempting offer it appears. I know it must seem to give you an easy way out of your difficulties, but you would do better to wait for me to find you a place—'

'As to that, I have already found one. Or rather, Mrs Pettifer has kindly found me one. The Hampsons are in need of someone to look after their children—'

'Pah! You can do better than looking after the Hampsons' children!'

'Indeed? So you forbid me to accept Mrs Hampson's offer as well? Tell me, Lord Carisbrooke, just whose offer will you allow me to accept?' she asked.

He took two steps towards her, and reaching down he cupped her face in his hands. 'You deserve better than a position with the Hampsons, worthy though they might be. But marriage to my cousin would not be better. There are things about Laurence you don't know.' His eyes darkened, as they had a habit of doing when he was moved. 'Laurence has no more right to offer you his hand than I have.'

His words were unexpected, and with a shock Hilary realized that his thoughts were wandering down their dark pathways again. Not being able to bear seeing him in pain she reached out impulsively, putting her hand on his arm. 'Something is hurting you,' she said. 'Won't you let me know what it is?'

He gave a deep sigh and for a moment she thought he was about to reveal his secret. Then he shook his grizzled head. 'No.'

'I want to help you,' she persisted.

He covered her small hand with his own. His touch was light and tender. Then he dropped his hand to his side.

'No one can help me,' he said in a hollow voice. 'Least of all you.' Again his mood had changed: it was as if he could not keep out the dark thoughts. His mood became grim. 'Except by going away from here.'

His words stung her. She had wanted to help him and he had rejected her. But still she could not let the matter rest. 'There is something wrong in the abbey,' she said, rising to her feet. 'I can feel it. It hangs over everything, making it dark and desperate. What is it, Marcus?'

But he ignored her question.

'Go to the Hampsons. Forget about this place,' he said, gripping her by the shoulders and looking deeply into her eyes.

'I can't.'

'You must.'

'Do you believe I can forget about the abbey, just because I go elsewhere? My memories do not shift and change with the passing scenery. They are etched into me. I cannot escape them by going elsewhere.'

'As to that, you will not be with them for long. I hope to find you a place in Bath, something more suited to your tastes and abilities. Once there, amongst the concert halls and pleasure gardens, mixing with cultivated and agreeable people, you will forget.'

'I will never forget,' she said, covering his hands with her own. 'Something is wrong here, I can feel it. It is eating you up from the inside. I cannot put it out of my mind. Just as I cannot put you out of my mind. You will be with me there, every bit as strongly as you are with me here.'

'You don't know what you are saying. You are young—'

'Not so young that my feelings will change.'

'I should never have let it come to this,' he said. 'It was wrong of me to allow you to stay in the abbey. I should have sent you away from here as soon as you arrived, but I let my surliness get the better of me. I refused to send you off in the carriage, and now I am repaid.'

'You are too hard on yourself. You did not know the river would flood overnight, or that the ford would become impassable.'

'Perhaps not. But I should have protected you from the abbey's influence all the same. Even when you were forced to stay under its roof I should have taken better care of you, sheltering you from its harsher realities. And I should not have kissed you.'

She felt him withdraw from her emotionally, as well as physically, as he dropped his hands. But she was not about to let him regret the most wonderful thing she had ever experienced.

'If you hadn't, I would have missed the most exhilarating sensations I have ever known. I never knew feelings like that existed
before I met you. You opened my eyes to a whole new world, and I
cannot regret it, even if you can. I will be glad you kissed me for the
rest of my life.'

'Oh, Hilary, if only—' he began, in anguish. Then his quicksilver
mood changed again. 'But it's impossible.'

'You are an earl, and I am forced to earn my own living—'

'Do you think I care for that?' he ground out. 'If it was only the
difference in our ranks, and nothing more, then I would clasp you to
me at once.'

'Then why—?'

'Don't ask me anything more. I cannot answer you.' He turned
away and strode across the room. He made a visible effort to control
himself. Then in a more normal voice he asked her, 'When are you
going to the Hampsons?'

'Tomorrow. They are to send the trap for me.'

'Good. The sooner you are away from the abbey the better. But
you cannot – shall not – limit yourself to a life of drudgery. I will
soon find you something better, a position that will give you room to
breathe, and I will send word to you as soon as I have found it.'

'Thank you.' She inclined her head. For although she was grateful
for the post with the Hampsons, it was only for a few weeks, or a
few months at most, and then she would have to have some other
way of supporting herself.

He gave her a burning look, as though he would like to take her
into his arms and rain kisses down on her. But instead he said, 'Go.
Go now.'

He turned his back on her.

She could see by the tautness of his stance that he was in the grip
of strong emotion. She had tried to reach him but she had failed. To
try again would only cause him more anguish. Whatever his burden

was, he was determined not to share it. And so she took pity on him.

Feeling every step an effort she left the room. It was as though her feet were made of lead.

CHAPTER NINE

*T*he clock chimed twelve as Hilary descended the magnificent staircase. She had shaken off the worst of her low spirits and recovered at least a little from her encounter with Lord Carisbrooke. But still she wondered what it was that haunted him, a secret so terrible he could not even bring himself to speak of it.

To divert her thoughts from their useless wanderings, she turned them to another mystery. Who had locked her outside on the roof? Could it really have been Mrs Lund? Or was there a more sinister explanation?

As she crossed the hall, she heard the tinkling sounds of the pianoforte coming from the direction of the cloisters. Evidently the Palmers were indulging in a little music before luncheon.

Could one of them have been responsible for her ordeal?

Her mind went back to the previous evening, when Lord Carisbrooke had kissed her in the library. There had been a clicking sound, as if the door had opened . . . or closed. What if Miss Palmer had seen them embracing, and had decided to remove Hilary as a rival? Would she go to those lengths to get what she wanted? Hilary wondered. Having met her, Hilary reluctantly thought it was possible.

Or could it have been Mrs Palmer? It might have been the older lady who had seen the embrace in the library. Then, catching sight of

Hilary going up to the attic, she might have followed her and given in to an impulse to get her out of the way by locking her on the roof. If so, was it a temporary or a permanent removal she had had in mind? For although Hilary had not been in any immediate danger, if she had not been found before nightfall she would almost certainly have died of the cold.

Or was she simply being fanciful? thought Hilary. Had it simply been an accident, with Lund or Mrs Lund locking her on the roof?

That was more probable. Still, until she knew for sure, she decided to be cautious, and to stay as far away from the Palmers as possible.

She turned her steps towards the library, but the fire had burned down low and the room was cold. She built it up with new logs and then made her way to the drawing-room, where she intended to sit until the library was warm enough for her to continue with her work. To her surprise, though, when she entered the drawing-room, it was not empty. Esmerelda was there, standing by the window, looking as lovely as ever.

She was dressed in more suitable fashion than the last time they had met. She was wearing a beautiful blue pelisse trimmed with swansdown, and on her feet were matching kid boots. Her elegant bonnet was tied beneath her chin with a blue ribbon, and it was decorated with a blue plume. Her hands were buried in a fashionable muff.

'Good morning,' said Esmerelda, turning round with a smile.

'Good morning,' said Hilary, quickly stifling her surprise. 'It is good to see you again.' Realizing that she was slipping into the role of hostess, which did not by rights belong to her, she asked, 'Does Lord Carisbrooke know you are here, or would you like me to tell him of your arrival?'

'That won't be necessary,' said Esmerelda with a bright smile. 'I have not come to see his lordship, I have come to see you.' She looked out of the window. 'The grounds are looking beautiful,' she said.

'They are,' Hilary agreed. 'Autumn suits them.'

'It does, doesn't it? The colours of the few remaining leaves look lovely against the sky. But you should see the gardens in the spring, when they are full of daffodils and crocuses, and later on they are better still, when the rhododendrons are out. There are pink ones and white ones and red ones. Blood red.'

'Unfortunately, I won't be here to see them.'

Esmerelda made no reply.

'Won't you take a seat?' asked Hilary. She guessed that Esmerelda, being a guest at the rectory, even if she was an unwanted one, must have come on an errand from Mrs Pettifer. She had some news about the Hampsons, perhaps. Hilary felt her spirits sink. Mayhap they could not take her today as arranged, and wanted to delay her appointment.

'No, thank you,' said Esmerelda. 'I won't be staying long.'

'How is Mrs Pettifer?'asked Hilary, not liking to take a seat herself as her guest had not done so.

'She's very well.'

'And Mr Pettifer? I hope he has recovered from his cold.'

'Oh, yes. It was nothing, you know. Men do so like to make a fuss!' said Esmerelda with a smile.

'Have you some word for me about the Hampsons? asked Hilary, when Esmerelda said nothing more.

'Not especially.' Esmerelda smiled brightly again. 'I wonder whether I might trouble you for some refreshment?'

She walked away from the window, into the centre of the room.

'Certainly.'

Hilary felt sure Lord Carisbrooke would want a guest from the rectory to be treated hospitably, especially as he himself had been so courteous to Mrs Pettifer. She went over to the mantelpiece to ring the bell.

As she did so the door opened.

Immediately the atmosphere changed, becoming thick and tinged with fear.

She looked towards the door in alarm, and saw Marcus standing there. On his face was a look of pain mingled with apprehension.

In a low, even voice, he said, 'Come over here to me, Hilary. Now.'

He did not look at her as he said it, but he kept his eyes fixed on Esmerelda.

Instinctively Hilary followed his gaze, and what she saw froze her blood. Esmerelda had taken her hands out of her muff, and she was holding a knife.

'Don't make any sudden movements,' said Marcus.

Hilary looked at Esmerelda again, and with a flash of understanding, she knew why Lord Carisbrooke was so afraid. There was a strange glitter in Esmerelda's eye. The beautiful young woman was insane.

Everything slipped into place: Esmerelda's unsuitable clothing the first time they had met; Marcus's reaction to finding Hilary alone in the folly; the strange conversation they had had the first night at dinner, when they had discussed the treatment of the mad; Marcus's warnings about being careful; the dark atmosphere that hung over the abbey; the pain that lay behind Marcus's eyes. All caused by this woman who was insane.

But what had she to do with Marcus?

Hilary had no time for further thought, because Esmerelda was taking a step towards her with the knife upraised. Slowly and carefully Hilary began to edge towards the door. Marcus was at the same time walking into the room, ready to shield her with his body if Esmerelda should strike.

And then it came. A sudden dart forward, a gleam of silver, the knife raised higher and then plunged down towards Hilary's breast.

But Marcus's hand was there, the long fingers wrapping themselves around Esmerelda's wrist as he gently but firmly prised the knife out of her hand.

'Are you all right?' he asked Hilary over his shoulder, when he had a firm grip on the knife.

'Perfectly.'

Her initial shock had passed, and she was once more in command of herself. She was no longer frightened. Instead she was concerned for Esmerelda. The elfin young woman was so lovely, and yet so tragically scarred. By now, however, Esmerelda had quietened. She had collapsed as soon as Marcus had taken the knife from her, falling into his arms like a puppet with cut strings.

'Here,' said Hilary.

She pulled forward an armchair.

Marcus guided Esmerelda towards it and pushed her gently into it. She offered no resistance and meekly sat down.

'I'm sorry,' Hilary said softly.

The words were inadequate, but she wanted him to know how much she felt for him in his tragic situation. She had seen a gleam of gold on Esmerelda's finger and realized, with a wrenching of her heart, that Esmerelda was Marcus's wife.

His eyes were tinged with a deep sadness. 'So am I.'

Their eyes held, and a world of communication passed between them.

Then Marcus knelt down in front of Esmerelda and spoke to her kindly, as though he was speaking to a child.

'That was very wrong of you, Esmerelda. You know you are not meant to leave the cottage when we have visitors. Why aren't you there?'

'I wanted someone to play with,' said Esmerelda plaintively.

'Then why bring the knife? You are not allowed to play with knives.'

She pouted.

'And where did you get it from? I thought Mrs Lund put all the knives away.'

Esmerelda's face became cunning. 'I'm not telling you.'

'Esmerelda,' he said sternly.

She grew petulant. 'No. You're not my friend. You took it away from me.'

'Is this how you were injured, on the night of the storm?' asked Hilary, as understanding began to dawn.

'Yes,' he said. 'Esmerelda is usually cared for by Mrs Lund, in a small cottage in the grounds, but she is afraid of thunderstorms and that night I brought her into the abbey. The hidden room behind the tapestry is kept ready for her, so that if she is ill or frightened she can be cared for there.'

'And she attacked you?' asked Hilary.

'She did. She was driven mad by the storm. Sometimes my presence soothes her, but on that occasion it enraged her. I returned to my room, but I had underestimated how weak I was from the loss of blood, and was near to collapsing when you found me.'

'And the scars above your eye?' asked Hilary softly. 'They, too, were made by Esmerelda.'

'They were.'

So much was now explained – even his tales of a ghostly abbess, which had evidently been designed to explain away any strange noises.

Esmerelda began to stir.

'I must get her out of the abbey,' he said. 'I cannot risk her being here. She might attack the Palmers – particularly Miss Palmer. If she sees other young ladies in the abbey she believes them to be usurpers, trying to take her place.'

'That is why you said you could not have a woman in the abbey,' said Hilary, at last understanding his strange words when she had arrived.

He nodded. 'It is dangerous, for even though Mrs Lund cares for her in the cottage she is cunning and sometimes manages to escape. But now I must get her back there. Her behaviour is unpredictable, and she could become violent again at any time.'

He stood up, still holding Esmerelda by the hand.

'Come, Esmerelda, let's go and find Lundy.' He turned to Hilary. 'Open the door for me.'

She was about to do as he said, when she heard the sound of footsteps on the other side.

'Someone to play with!' said Esmerelda, struggling to get free.

'Hell's teeth!' said Marcus. He glanced at the fireplace. 'Over there,' he said. 'The wall sconce by the fireplace. Pull it down.'

Hilary was unsurprised at the strange command. She had seen from the plans in the library that the abbey contained a number of secret passages, and she guessed that this was how the one in the drawing-room was accessed. Hurrying over to the fireplace, she took a firm grip on the wall sconce and pulled it downwards. A concealed door at the side of the fireplace swung open.

Holding the struggling, spitting Esmerelda tightly, Marcus manoeuvred her into the secret passage, then closed the door behind him by way of a lever in the passage. The wall sconce, complete with candle, resumed its proper place. And not a moment too soon. The drawing-room door opened, and Mrs and Miss Palmer entered.

Miss Palmer stopped dead. She looked displeased to see Hilary. Recovering herself somewhat, she said suspiciously, 'I thought I heard voices.'

Hilary replied calmly, 'As you can see, I am alone.'

'And up to no good, I imagine,' said Miss Palmer maliciously.

'Indeed,' said her mother. 'Skulking here in the drawing-room by the best fire when you have work to do. Lord Carisbrooke appointed you to organize his library, girl, not to make yourself at home in the drawing-room. I suggest you get on with it, before I tell him what you are about.'

'With pleasure,' said Hilary.

'Really!' said Mrs Palmer, as Hilary left the room. 'What impertinence!'

'I shall tell Lord Carisbrooke to give her her notice,' said Miss Palmer.

'Gentlemen! They know nothing of household matters. Imagine appointing a chit of a girl to a post as a librarian, when a presentable young gentleman would have been so much better.'

Hilary closed the door behind her, glad to be out of their presence.

She went to the library, which she knew would be a haven of peace and quiet. She looked around at the unsorted shelves, and at the books on the table that she had started to sort on the previous day. She ought to continue. The familiar work would soothe her nerves. But she felt disinclined to continue. She went over to the window, and stood looking out over the grey gardens. Now she understood Lord Carisbrooke's nature, and the cause of his pain. She also understood his contradictory attitude towards her. He was attracted to her, both to her personality and her person. But he could not follow his inclinations, because he was married.

What torments he must have suffered, thought Hilary, as she gazed unseeing over the abbey grounds. What terrible pain. To be married to a wife who was beautiful and clearly dear to him, but who was insane.

She felt an overwhelming sympathy for him, as she thought of what he had had to bear. And he had borne it uncomplainingly. He was a man of great strength of character, but even so, his secret had tried him to his limits. And yet he had kept it, rather than burden her with the truth.

She wandered over to the fire. Caesar lay there with his head on his paws. As she approached, he got up and stood beside her, knocking her hand with his head.

Interpreting the gesture correctly, she stroked his soft fur. The feel of it brought her some comfort. Here, at least, was something uncomplicated. The simple action was soothing, and gradually she began to feel calmer.

At last she let her eyes roam round the library. She still felt disinclined to work, and yet she must do something to rouse herself from the melancholy that threatened to overtake her. Her eye came to rest on one of the books which she had dusted the previous day. It was very old, and contained a number of plans of the abbey. It was in this book that she had seen the secret passages.

She went over to the bookshelves and took it out, carrying it over to the fire. Sitting herself down in a wing chair she opened it and examined the plans. There were a number of secret passages marked. She found the one in the drawing-room and traced it with her finger. Before it reached its other end, she had already guessed where it would come out: in the room behind the tapestry.

And there Marcus was now, if she did not miss her guess, caring for Esmerelda.

This new development caused Hilary pain. Her feelings were deep and sincere, but they were not the sort of feelings she should allow herself to entertain towards a married man. And yet it was difficult for her to hide from them. Lord Carisbrooke was the most compelling man she had ever met. She respected and admired him for carrying his burden uncomplainingly, and for looking after his poor, damaged wife in the abbey instead of sending her to an asylum where she would be beaten and chained. And she felt a profound friendship for him.

If her feelings had gone no further, then she would have been comfortable. Respect, admiration and friendship were perfectly permissible in relation to a married man.

But her other feelings were not so comfortable. She must not encourage the warm and tender feelings she had for him, which led her to want to take him in her arms and comfort him, not only with soothing words but with caresses. Nor must she allow herself to think of the other feelings she had for him, the feelings that rejoiced whenever he took her into his arms. His kisses had been breathtaking; wonderful.

But she must never feel them again. They were dishonourable. They demeaned him. They demeaned her. And they demeaned poor, damaged Esmerelda.

She tried hard to banish them. But whilst it was one thing for her head to decide that she should not feel these things, it was another for her heart to manage it.

She closed the book.

She should get up, busy herself, go about her work, but she could not move. She could only think of Marcus, and her feelings for him. They had been gradually growing, until now she was no longer in any doubt about their nature.

She was in love with him.

She had never thought love would be like this. She had thought it would be like a childhood birthday, exciting and pleasurable but ultimately superficial.

But it was not. Her love for Marcus was as deep as the ocean. It was as strong as the earth. It encompassed every emotion and every passion, filling every corner of her life. It was composed of esteem, friendship, approbation, and comfort, all being intuitively given and received. It was desire and passion, longing and yearning. And it was a calling of the spirit, his to hers, and hers to his.

But it could never be fulfilled.

Not for her.

Not for Marcus.

Because Esmerelda was his wife.

With a heavy heart, Hilary forced herself to stand. She made her legs carry her over to the bookcase. And she began to work.

She did so slowly to begin with, but gradually with more decision, as the activity gave her an outlet for her feelings. She carried and dusted, sorted and organized, attacking the shelves with vigour. By and by, the sorted shelves grew in number, and the unsorted shelves shrank.

She had almost finished the second bookcase when all her good intentions to forget about Marcus were blown away, because he walked into the library.

He was looking pale, and his face was drawn. There was a tired set to his head, and his shoulders drooped.

She longed to comfort him. She wanted to pull out a chair and push him gently into it, to stroke his grizzled hair and soothe him with soft words and gentle caresses.

But she could not do it.

To make sure that she did not forget her good resolution she remained behind the table, where the solid oak and the pile of books formed a barrier between them, and spoke determinedly of Esmerelda.

'How is she?' she asked.

As if sensing her need for a barrier, he did not draw any closer. Instead, he stood just within the room.

'She's calm,' he said. His eyes turned to hers. 'I owe you an explanation.'

'You owe me nothing,' she returned gently.

His voice was hollow. 'I should have told you the truth when I knew you would have to remain here for some days. It was not safe for me to withhold it.'

'I should have done as you bid me,' she countered, refusing to let him take the blame. 'If I had stayed in the abbey I would not have been at risk. Esmerelda would not have seen me in the grounds, and if she had not known of my existence she would not have tried to kill me. But she seemed so normal, I never suspected. And I have done other reprehensible things.' She took a deep breath. 'I have encouraged—'

'Never encouraged,' he interrupted softly.

'Then allowed you to kiss me,' she continued. 'But I never dreamed you had a wife.'

'A wife?'

'I saw the wedding band on her finger,' Hilary explained.

He let out a deep sigh. 'I see.'

He took a step forward.

Hilary braced herself against the table.

And then a voice from the hall interrupted them.

'Have you seen Miss Wentworth, Lund?'

'Laurence!' cursed Marcus. 'Are we never to get any peace? This is what comes of having guests in the abbey. Meet me in the folly,' he growled, glancing out of the window and seeing that the weather was fine. 'I must speak to you, but I cannot do it here for fear of interruptions. I want you to myself. Come as quickly as you can.'

She nodded. There was time for nothing more. The door was already opening and Laurence, beautifully attired in cream breeches, a blue tailcoat, white shirt and expertly arranged cravat, with highly polished Hessians adorning his small feet, was walking into the room.

'Ah! Miss—' he began with a smile, as his eyes fell on Hilary. Then he saw his cousin. 'Marcus,' he said stiffly.

'Laurence. I was just leaving.'

Laurence bowed.

Marcus left the room.

'Miss Wentworth. I am pleased to have found you.' A slight frown wrinkled his brow. 'Though I am not pleased to have found you at work. That, I hope, will soon be a thing of the past. I have come to ask you if you have had time to consider my proposal.'

Hilary gave an inward sigh. She really did not want to speak to Mr Ulverstone now, but it could not be avoided. Besides, she owed him a polite and final rejection of his hand. 'I have. I am very flattered by your offer, and sensible of the great honour you do me by making it, but I am sorry, I cannot marry you. My answer must still be "no".'

His brow darkened. 'I don't like to think of you at the Hampsons,' he said. 'They are ignorant people, and you will have no one to indulge your love of good conversation. Neither Mr nor Mrs Hampson play chess or cards, and I cannot see anything for you there but stagnation. Is my offer really so abhorrent to you that you would prefer a life of servitude?'

'Your offer is a very attractive one, but I have to refuse it because I do not love you,' she said gently. 'I know some people marry without love, and even that they go on to lead happy lives, but that is not for me. I could not marry a man I did not love, no matter how appealing my life might be afterwards.'

'I see.'

'I hope you do,' she said softly.

'Ah, well.' His brow cleared. 'I cannot force you to marry me, nor indeed would I want to. I hope you will be – I was going to say happy: I do not believe that is possible; but at least not unhappy – with the Hampsons.'

'As to that, I don't believe I will be with them for very long. Lord Carisbrooke has kindly offered to exert his influence, and find me a position in Bath.'

'Good.' He looked relieved. 'That is better than you remaining here. But even so, I will give you my direction. If you change your mind, a letter will bring me to you at any time.'

'You are very good.'

'I fear not,' he said, with a wry smile. 'Selfishness is my motivation, and not goodness.'

He took out a card and handed it to her.

'I wish you well, Miss Wentworth, whatever your future holds,' he said.

'And I you.'

'Then we part as friends,' he said with a smile.

'Indeed we do.'

He made her a bow and left the room.

Hilary glanced at the card, which contained his name and address, and saw that he lived in Upper Brook Street. It was a fashionable and expensive part of London. If she had been able to accept his hand she would have been going there this afternoon, instead of to a local farmer's house. But she did not regret her decision.

She waited only for his footsteps to recede before she slipped upstairs, dropped the card on the dressing-table, threw on her pelisse, and headed for the folly.

She should not be doing it, said her head. She should be avoiding Marcus. No good could come of meeting him. But her feet took her onwards, speeding across the lawns and threading her way through the shrubbery until at last she emerged in sight of the folly.

She stopped.

She was suddenly afraid.

If she went any further she would be alone with Marcus and there would be no chance of interruption. If their passions should get the better of them . . . . She lifted her chin. She must make sure they did not.

She went forward again, more slowly now, approaching the ruined temple. It was exactly as she remembered it. Its ruined walls looked ghostly in the November light.

At first she thought Marcus had not come. But then she saw him emerging from the ruin. Every line of him was dear to her: his shaggy hair, his deep-set eyes, his strong features, and his bear-like frame. She felt a tug towards him as if she was being drawn towards a lode-stone and fought it with all her might. If she went to him now she would fly into his arms. And so she resisted the pull, looking at him across the clearing, drinking him in.

He was the first to break the silence that stretched between them.

'You came.'

She nodded. She did not trust herself to speak.

His hand raised. 'I want you so much . . .'

She could tell he needed to touch her. And she needed him to. She needed to feel him running his hand over her face, and then turn her cheek against it, luxuriating in his caress.

But it could not be.

He let his hand fall. 'I can never have you,' he said.

She could tell how desperately he wanted to close the distance between them. She could see him trembling with tension as he willed himself to stay where he was.

She must help him; remind him why they must remain apart.

'But you are married,' she whispered.

'No.'

She barely heard the word, for he had stepped towards her. He had abandoned the fight and given in to the attraction between them.

He raised his hand again and this time he was close enough to stroke her cheek.

She felt her mouth go dry. She should shake him off. But it felt so wonderful that she did not have the will to do it.

'I am not married,' he said.

This time, his words registered. He must be married. She had seen Esmerelda's ring.

'Esmerelda—' she said.

'—is not my wife.'

'*Not* . . . ?'

Hilary stared. She thought he had said Esmerelda was not his wife. But she must have misheard him. Her senses, clouded by his touch, were not to be trusted.

'Esmerelda is my sister,' he said softly.

'Your sister?'

'Yes.'

'But the ring—'

'Was my mother's. She left it to Esmerelda when she died.'

Hilary felt the first stirrings of hope growing inside her.

'Then . . . .'

'Then we are free to marry?' He finished the sentence for her. 'No, my love, we are not.'

Her spirits sank. 'I don't understand.'

'In a way, I wish Esmerelda was my wife. Then, at least in the future, we might have a chance of happiness, you and I.'

Hilary's confusion was written across her face.

'This has all been very sudden,' he said. 'You have not yet had a chance to understand what it means.'

He took her arm and led her inside the ruined temple. Large stones, arranged with apparent negligence, formed a perfect seat.

She sank down on to the mossy stone.

He sat beside her.

He took her hands and looked into her eyes.

'My father was mad. My sister is mad. And one day I, too, will be mad. And that is why I can never marry you.'

She gave a deep sigh. So this was the terrible secret that haunted the abbey. At last she understood.

But it did not change her feelings for him.

'It is a terrible misfortune,' she said, 'but it does not make any difference. I love you, Marcus. I love you sane, and I will love you insane. Did you really believe it would be otherwise?'

He gave a bleak smile. 'No. I knew it would not.'

'I will look after you, care for you—'

'My love, I could never allow it. I know what agonies you would suffer. I saw my mother suffer them as my father went mad. I saw her fear; I saw her anguish; I saw her pity.'

'It is true I might come to fear you, and I might also pity you, but you are forgetting that I would also love you.'

He took her hands in his.

'God bless you for that. But even so, it can never be. You do not know what will happen. My behaviour will become unpredictable, and in the end it will become violent. I might attack you, or even kill you.'

'But this is all in the future,' she protested. 'We would have some time together first. Weeks, months, perhaps even years.'

He stroked her palms with his thumbs.

'We would. And if it was only the two of us I would fly in the face of fate and take you to wife whilst I can. But it would not only be the two of us. There would be children from our union, and they, too, would be tainted with insanity. You would not only have to watch your husband turn into a beast, but you would have to watch your children sink into madness as well.'

It was a bleak picture, and despite herself she trembled.

Even so, her love for him was strong.

'We would not have to have children,' she ventured. 'I feel things for you that I do not fully understand. When you take me into your arms my thoughts become confused, and I find myself longing for things I have never experienced. But these feelings are only a small part of my love for you. I would be happy just being with you, your friend and your helpmeet. And, in time, your nurse.'

He spoke gently. 'I know. I have thought of this, too. If we had separate rooms . . . but with only a corridor between us, in the end, I would give way to my feelings.'

'I could lock my door,' she said.

'It would do no good.' His voice was throaty. 'Once you were my wife, no lock would keep me out.'

She knew the truth of it. Even if she could find the will to lock her door, he would break it down.

And she would want him to.

Her heart misgave her. There was nothing ahead of her but emptiness, and her spirit quailed at the thought of it.

'Then there is no hope,' she whispered.

His fingers wrapped around her own, squeezing them tightly.

'None.'

Her world collapsed. That final word, bereft of optimism, was like a death knell.

She felt his arm slip round her shoulder, and with a sigh she leant against him as he cradled her to his chest. These were the last private moments they would share, and she would have to make their tenderness last a lifetime.

'I had hoped to spare you this,' he said at last, as he pulled away from her. 'I wanted you to leave the abbey and forget me.'

'I'm glad you didn't. These few days have meant more to me than the rest of my life. And I'm glad I know you love me. At least now, I can understand.'

'Perhaps you are right. Perhaps it is better this way.'

He turned to face her. 'Then one last kiss,' he said softly.

He bent his head and kissed her sweetly on the lips.

All his feelings were pouring out of him, and she felt them all; all his love for her, and his longing, and his regret that things could not be any other way.

At last he let her go.

She did not want him to. She wanted the kiss to go on for ever. But although her heart cried out against its ending, she knew they must stop now, whilst they still could.

But still they could not separate.

They sat there, fingers entwined, in the wintry light, together and yet apart. Their bodies were as one, their hearts and their spirits, but soon they must go their different ways.

The clock on the stables chimed the hour, then the half hour, but still they did not move. The air grew cold. Rain began to fall.

At last Marcus stirred. 'We must go in.'

Her heart misgave her. This was where it began, the final separation. But it must be done. She stood up slowly, painfully, with every movement an effort. Marcus rose beside her and they walked back to the abbey.

They did not touch. They did not speak. Yet they were bound together, by love and sorrow.

As they entered the hall, Marcus turned towards her.

'I will leave you here,' he said.

Hilary nodded. She did not trust herself to speak.

Then he turned away from her, leaving her standing there, desolate and alone.

Finally she roused herself and went upstairs. She removed her pelisse and bonnet, laying them on the bed. Then a great weariness overtook her and she lay down beside them.

How long she lay there she did not know, but at last she began to shake off some of her listlessness. She knew she must get up, for she had much to do. Her body felt heavy, but she managed to rise from her bed. She went over to the washstand, where she washed her face in order to refresh herself, and then set about packing her few possessions so that she would be ready when the Hampsons' trap should call. She folded her dowdy dresses and stowed them away in her portmanteau, together with her soft indoor shoes, her underwear and her shawl, before putting her brush and comb on top of them. She added her book then glanced round the room to make sure she had not forgotten anything. There was a card on the table. She picked it up and frowned. Howard and Gibbs, she read. The name looked familiar, but she could not place it. How had she come by the card? she wondered. Then her expression cleared, and turning it over she saw that it was Mr Ulverstone's card.

Did he need the names scrawled on the back? she wondered.

Perhaps she had better ask him.

She was just about to go in search of him when she heard a crunching of gravel outside. She went over to the window, expecting to see the Hampsons' trap, but saw instead Mr Ulverstone's coach. It was too late to return the card, but she doubted the names were important. If they had been, he would have taken more care of them. It was strange, though. They seemed familiar. She had the feeling her uncle had mentioned them at some time. In which case, they were probably the name of his favourite London bootmakers.

If she had accepted Mr Ulverstone's hand she could have been leaving in fine style, she reflected, going to a new life of luxury and affluence in the heart of London's most fashionable district. But she did not regret her decision. She could never have made Mr Ulverstone happy, and he could never have made her anything but grateful. And gratitude was no substitute for love.

As she watched, the luggage was loaded and Mr Ulverstone appeared. To Hilary's surprise, he had Miss Palmer on one arm and Mrs Palmer on the other. But a moment's reflection showed her that it was not so very surprising after all. There was still a threat of rain in the air, and he had evidently offered to take them home. It was truly kind of him, thought Hilary, as Miss Palmer would no doubt set her cap at him now that she had not been successful in her pursuit of Lord Carisbrooke, and he would have to tolerate her coquetry until he deposited her at her home.

Hilary's thoughts turned once again to Marcus. It was not wise of her to stay in the same neighbourhood, but until he could arrange another position for her elsewhere, or she could discover one for herself, then she would have to do so.

The coach rolled away, just as the Hampsons' trap came down the drive.

She slipped into her pelisse, then settled her bonnet on her head. She tied the strings under her chin before pulling on her gloves.

There came a knock at the door.

Her heart jumped.

But it was only Lund, come to carry her portmanteau.

She followed him down the wide, shallow stairs, taking in the stately grandeur for the last time.

At the bottom of the stairs stood Marcus.

She was glad he had come to say goodbye. She had thought that, under the circumstances, he might think it wiser to avoid her, but he was there waiting for her.

Her eyes ran over him, committing every line of his face to memory.

He might not be handsome, but she could never have such profound feelings for anyone else. Every feature was etched with character. His charcoal eyes, his strong nose and his decided chin, all told of his uncompromising character and his enduring nature.

As she came to a halt three steps above him, so that they were face to face, she looked deeply into his eyes. She wished she could have healed his wounds and lightened his burden. Instead she feared she had made it heavier by showing him a glimpse of what he could not have.

But as he took her hand and kissed it, she knew it was not so.

'I don't regret a moment,' he said to her, his voice low and husky.

She took comfort from his words. 'Neither do I.'

Then, descending the final few steps she left the abbey behind her and went out to the waiting trap.

CHAPTER TEN

'I'm bringing forward my visit to Lyme.'

It was the morning after Hilary had left the abbey, and Marcus was speaking to Mrs Lund. He was restless, and in low spirits. He had parted with the only woman he had ever loved, and the thought of it was driving him to distraction. He was tempted, every minute of the day, to ride over to the Hampsons and ask Hilary to spend what little time he had left with him. Moreover, he was afraid that if he did not go away at once, he would probably do it.

'Very good, my lord,' said Mrs Lund. 'Will you be leaving straight away?'

'Just as soon as I can pack my things.' He turned penetrating eyes on her. 'You will be able to manage whilst I am gone?'

'Yes, my lord. Esmerelda won't be any trouble now that Lund's put a bolt on the outside of the cottage door. Even if she manages to pick the lock again, she won't be able to get out.'

'I hate treating her like this,' he said with a sigh. 'Last time she escaped I had to get Lund to put bars on the windows and this time it's a bolt on the outside of the door. I feel I'm making a prisoner of her, but it has to be done. She is becoming increasingly cunning, and increasingly violent. Are you sure you can manage her? I can hire a nurse to help you if you would like. I don't want you to come to any harm.'

'Esmerelda would never hurt me,' said Mrs Lund. 'She still has a hazy memory of coming into the kitchen when she was a little girl and helping me with the baking. She'd take a turn with the rolling; pin and help to put the filling in the pies.

' "There's not enough pastry to make another one", I'd say, "but I don't like to waste this bit that's left. If only I'd someone to eat it for me, I could use it up in a jam tart". There's many a tart she's eaten to help me use up the pastry!'

Marcus smiled. Esmerelda might have descended into madness but she had a devoted nurse in Mrs Lund.

Then his smile faded.

'I've taken every precaution I can think of, but I'm still concerned about her getting out again,' he said.

'She'll be all right now the visitors have gone,' said Mrs Lund. 'It's just having people in the abbey that unsettles her, particularly if they're young ladies.'

'You've locked away all the knives?' he asked.

'I have,' said Mrs Lund. 'Even if she escapes again, and makes her way to the kitchen, she won't be able to find anything sharp.'

'Good.'

'You'll see,' said Mrs Lund. 'Now that the visitors have gone she'll soon settle down again. I left her with Lund, happily playing with her dolls.'

Marcus nodded. Esmerelda was always more unpredictable when the abbey had guests.

'Will you say goodbye to her?' asked Mrs Lund.

Marcus pursed his lips. 'No. The knowledge that I'm leaving might unsettle her. It will be better for her if she doesn't know I'm going away.'

Mrs Lund nodded. 'I think that's best.'

'Well, I mustn't keep you. You will be wanting to get back to her. Send Lund to me, will you, when you have relieved him? I will need him to help me pack.'

Mrs Lund inclined her head and left the room.

Marcus watched her go. Then he turned his attention back to his own affairs.

His visit to Lyme was a regular occurrence, and had been so for five years. He went to visit his mother's nurse, an elderly lady by the name of Miss Maud Simmons, who had retired there following his mother's death. In appreciation of his thanks for her long service and her loyalty, Marcus had bought her a house in Lyme, and she now resided there with her widowed sister, Yvonne.

His visits usually took place in March, June, September and December, but he felt trapped in the abbey and bringing forward his winter visit would give him a good excuse to escape.

He had already given instructions in the stables that the coach was to be readied, and as soon as Lund had packed his trunk he was on his way.

Hilary's first few days at the Hampsons' farmhouse were thankfully busy ones, and she threw herself into her new life in an effort to dismiss Marcus from her mind.

When she had arrived at the farmhouse, she had been pleased to find that it was clean and welcoming, but without an active mistress it was beginning to show signs of disorder. The three lively children had been running wild, and Hannah, the maid, had been so busy chasing them round the house that her work was being left half done.

Now, four days after Hilary had arrived, some semblance of order had been restored.

'Lift your leg, dear,' she said to five-year-old Mary as she helped her step into her pantalettes.

'Don't want to,' said Mary rebelliously, putting her thumb in her mouth.

'Miss Wentworth,' called nine-year-old Sara from across the bedroom. 'I can't find my sash.'

'I'll help you in a minute,' said Hilary, praying for patience, before giving her attention back to Mary. 'Come, now, Mary, if you don't hurry up, your mother will be wondering where we are.'

It was her custom to take the girls in to see their mother for a short time every morning and afternoon, but this simple activity required all her organizational ability.

'Come, now, Mary, lift your leg,' she said more sternly.

Mary sucked her thumb mutinously, but at last gave in.

Just as Hilary had pulled on the frilly pantalette and was about to tie the tapes, a loud shriek rent the air.

'My sash!'

Hilary looked up to see Sara chasing eight-year-old Janet over the beds, whilst Janet clutched the scarlet sash.

'Give it to me!' shouted Sara.

Janet laughed impishly. Glancing over her shoulder to stick out her tongue at her sister she failed to see the stool in her path and fell over it with a crash. There was a stunned silence, and then she began to wail.

Hilary sighed. The girls had been unsettled by the new baby's arrival and were difficult to control.

Gradually she restored order. She dried Janet's eyes, tied Sara's sash and fastened Mary's pantalette then, having succeeded in making all three girls presentable, she took them in to see their mother.

Mrs Hampson, lying in after the birth of her latest child, was dressed in a white cotton nightdress, with a woollen shawl around her shoulders and a frilled cap on her head. The birth had been easy and she was feeling quite well, so that she was delighted to see the children.

The three girls lost no time in scrambling on to her bed, making loud complaints against each other. Once they had been alternately soothed and chastised, their high spirits gradually subsided, and they wandered over to the crib, where they amused themselves by arguing over their baby sister.

'I think I'll get up tomorrow,' said Mrs Hampson, turning her eyes from her children and giving her attention to Hilary.

'But surely the doctor said—'

'You can't go listening to what Dr Harris says,' said Mrs Hampson blithely. 'These doctors don't know anything. I'm perfectly well. Besides, there's nothing to do in bed.'

'Perhaps, for a short while . . .' began Hilary.

'That's just what I think. I'll get up tomorrow morning. It's one thing Hannah bringing me all the news, it's another being up and hearing it for myself. Did you know, Lord Carisbrooke's left the abbey?'

Hilary was startled. 'No. I didn't.'

'Oh, yes. Hannah had it from her mother, who had it from Mrs Potter, whose youngest, Duncan, is a stable boy at the abbey,' Mrs Hampson said. 'But never mind, he won't be gone for long. If he promised to find you a position, then he'll find you one, you mark my words.'

Hilary had told Mrs Hampson of Lord Carisbrooke's exertions on her behalf which had soothed the kindly, if garrulous, woman's fears.

'He's never gone for very long,' continued Mrs Hampson. 'He goes to Lyme to visit his mother's old nurse. There's many in the village as says strange things about the abbey, but they read too many novels, that's what my Peter says, and I'm sure he must be right, for some of the things they say are more like the things in a book, strange noises and mad people and secret passages and ghosts. They used to dare each other to go up there and spend a night in the grounds. Reading too much Mrs Radcliffe, that's what my Peter thinks. Do you like Mrs Radcliffe?' she asked, going off on a sudden tangent.

'Indeed I do,' said Hilary, grateful to be able to turn the conversation away from Marcus. 'I am reading *The Mysteries of Udolpho* at the moment.'

'Isn't it horrid?' said Mrs Hampson with round eyes. 'I keep trying to give it to Sara, but she won't take an interest.'

She looked at Sara and sighed.

Hilary suppressed a smile as she privately reflected that nine-year-old Sara was rather too young for *The Mysteries of Udolpho*!

'She was a lovely woman, Lady Carisbrooke's nurse,' said Mrs Hampson. 'We used to see her in church. Nothing high and mighty about her, even though she was so well thought of by the family. Lord Carisbrooke goes to see her as regular as clockwork, four times a year. Now that shows how well he thinks of her. She was a comfort to his mother, poor lady, losing her husband and then having her daughter so ill. Did you see Lady Esmerelda at the abbey?' asked Mrs Hampson.

'I . . .' Hilary was not sure what to say.

'Such a bright thing she used to be, before she got brought so low. We used to see her at church all the time, and she used to go to neighbourhood parties. But all that had to stop, of course, when she got ill. Consumption, I think it is, or some other such thing. We never see her now. She's confined to the abbey, poor young lady.'

So this was the reason Marcus had given for his sister's withdrawal from local life, Hilary reflected. And indeed, it was partly the truth, for she was indeed ill.

She remembered the way in which Mrs Pettifer had reacted when she had said that Esmerelda was a guest at the rectory. From Mrs Pettifer's startled glance, and from the way Mrs Pettifer had helped her to find another position, Hilary guessed that the rector's wife suspected the real nature of Esmerelda's illness, even if no one else did.

At that moment, Janet pulled Mary's hair and Mrs Hampson's

attention was distracted, so that fortunately Hilary was not called upon to say any more about Esmerelda.

'I'll take the children up to the schoolroom,' said Hilary.

'Oh, yes, do,' said Mrs Hampson, lying back against her pillows. 'I'm ever so tired all of a sudden. But bring them to see me again this afternoon.'

The girls set up a wail, but at last Hilary managed to manoeuvre them out of the room and take them up to the attic, where she settled them down to work. As their protests gave way to the sound of chalk on slates, she found her thoughts wandering. They were not with the Hampson girls in the low room with its cosy cream paint-work and its bright rug on the floor: they were with Marcus.

Marcus looked down at Lyme from his vantage point on top of the cliffs. He had ordered his coachman to stop in a fit of restlessness and had climbed out, walking to the edge of the cliffs in order to survey the scene. It was bleak, and yet its familiarity and pleasant memories soothed his troubled spirit.

Below him, the grey sea was choppy. It was dotted with boats riding the waves, which were being whipped into white peaks by the wind. His eyes moved inland, coming to rest on the Cobb. A few hardy souls were walking along its length. There was a solitary gentleman on the upper Cobb, and on the lower Cobb there were two gentlemen supporting their wives as they hurried along, the ladies holding on to their bonnets to prevent them from blowing away.

He turned his attention to the beach. A little boy, his trouser legs rolled up to his knees, was running across the sand before presenting his mother with a strand of seaweed, which she took as though it had been as precious as a string of pearls. Nearby, a labourer was strug-gling to remove an abandoned bathing machine.

Marcus felt some of the tension leave his shoulders. The familiar sights, together with the tang of salt, were working their magic. He was glad he had brought forward his visit. In the abbey, his thoughts had been too full of Hilary, but here he had a chance to distract them, even if it was only for a short while.

His eyes wandered to the houses that clustered beneath him in picturesque confusion. Their stone walls and pitched roofs were rugged, and fitted in well with the seaside scene. He picked out the one belonging to Maud, who had been his mother's nurse, and then his.

Reminded of his reason for the visit, he returned to the coach, the wind blowing his caped greatcoat round his ankles as he did so. He was soon on his way.

His arrival in the main street caused many a curious glance. Visitors were not common at this time of year, particularly visitors with coats of arms on their coaches, but their curiosity quickly gave way to recognition. His visits, whilst infrequent, were regular, and he was a familiar sight in Lyme.

The coach finally pulled up before his nurse's door.

The curtain twitched and he caught a glimpse of Yvonne, his nurse's sister, before the curtain fell back into place again. He growled with pleasure as he imagined the bustle that would be taking place inside the house: the instructions to the maid, the plumping of cushions, and the examination of the larder to see if there was any cake to be had. His nurse and her sister had always been very particular about the receiving of guests, and earl or rector, the preparations were always the same.

He climbed out of the carriage slowly, giving them time to attend to the small details that meant a great deal to them, then opened the gate and went up the path to the door.

Everything seemed to be in good order. The gate was newly painted, and the worn timbers in the door had been replaced. Those had been the things he had seen to on his last visit. But a rattling sound drew his attention upwards. One of the windows was fitting loosely, and would need attention if it was to keep out draughts. He would have to give instructions for it to be taken care of before he left.

He rapped on the door and a minute later it opened, to reveal a white-haired old woman. She was wearing a high-necked grey gown with a cameo pinned at the throat. The cameo had been left to her by his mother, and she wore it every day. She had a large shawl wrapped round her shoulders, and on her nose was a pair of *pince-nez*.

'Marcus, my dear, what a pleasant surprise!' She spoke to him as though he was still seven years old. 'We didn't expect you for another three weeks. But don't stand out there in the cold, come in.'

The door was low. He had to stoop to pass through it, and remain stooping as he went through the hall, but once in the parlour he could straighten up to his full height. It was just as he remembered it. There was gold paint on the walls, and a large brick fireplace with a healthy fire. His eyes swept the room to make sure there were no signs of neglect on the part of the maid, but evidently she looked after her mistresses well. The fire irons were polished, and the brass scuttle on the hearth was full of coal. The knick-knacks that cluttered the three small tables, including silhouettes of his mother, Esmerelda and himself, were properly dusted. The carpet was swept, and the sprigged curtains hanging at the windows were freshly laundered.

He was satisfied.

'Let me take your coat. I have rung for the maid, but she is seeing to the chickens and it might take her a minute or two to get here. It is such a pleasure to see you,' she said, as she took his coat from him and went out into the hall, returning a minute later without it.

'We did not look for you so soon,' said Yvonne. She was a small, round lady, with sparkling eyes and hair even whiter than her sister's.

Her ruby-red gown strained at the seams, but the creaking of corsets showed that she had not yet abandoned all hopes of taming her figure. 'That makes this a double treat.'

The two ladies sat down, and Marcus followed suit, settling himself in a comfortable armchair by the fire.

'I hope I haven't put you out?' he asked.

'You could never put us out, dear.'

Marcus smiled. Just for the moment he did not mind being treated as though he was a small boy. It took him back to happier times, and it was balm to his troubled spirit.

The door opened and the young maid hurried in.

'Yes, your lordship? What can I get you, your lordship?' she said breathlessly, making Marcus an awkward curtsy.

'There is no need to curtsy, Poll,' said his nurse kindly to the girl. 'And you should still address your mistresses, even if there is an earl in the room.'

'Yes, my lady, I mean Miss Maud,' said the girl, flustered.

'We will have our tea now,' she said.

Bobbing another curtsy, the girl left the room.

'How are you finding her?' asked Marcus, amused. 'Is she efficient? She seems eager to please, at least.'

'She is,' said Maud with a twinkle. 'She is a dear girl and looks after us very well, even if she is rather overawed by your visit!'

'It is not to be wondered at,' said Yvonne. 'It is not every day she sees such a splendid coach drawing up in front of the house, particularly not one with a coat of arms on the door. In fact, as she is new, she has never seen it happen before. She will have something to tell her mother when she goes home this evening, that's for sure!'

Marcus smiled. Satisfied that everything was as it should be, he leaned back in his chair and stretched out his legs to the fire.

'You both look well,' he said.

'We are. Yvonne had a chill a few weeks ago—'

'Really, Maud, it was nothing,' protested Yvonne.

'But she has thrown it off,' continued Maud, unperturbed. 'The air here is wonderful, and we make the most of it by walking along the Cobb every day.'

'I noticed several people out walking as I arrived, though it hardly seems the weather for it.'

'Nonsense! There is nothing wrong with the weather. It is bracing,' declared Maud.

She took up her knitting.

'What are you making?' he asked her.

'A blanket for old Mr Johnson.'

'Old Mr Johnson is five years younger than you are!' he smiled.

'That's as may be, but his knees are troubling him and he has to keep them warm. Besides, it gives me something to do.'

'You are not too dull here?' he asked.

'No, indeed. We have all the interest of the guests in the summer, and then there are the assemblies and the balls. We like to see the young people enjoying themselves! Then, too, we have made so many friends here. There are the Johnsons, and the Westons and the Armitages. Lyme suits us very well.' She looked up from her knitting, and pushed her *pince-nez* further up her nose. 'Now, tell me, how are things at the abbey?'

Marcus shifted uncomfortably in his seat.

'How is Esmerelda?'

Marcus's shoulders slumped. Thoughts of his sister were not happy ones. 'No better.'

Maud spoke softly. 'It is not to be expected. But is she happy?'

'Yes, in her own way, I believe she is.'

'Then that is all we can hope for.' Her eyes wandered to the silhouette of Esmerelda on the table, and she sighed.

'And the Lunds?' she asked, returning her attention to her knitting. 'They are keeping well?'

'Yes. Lund grumbles constantly, as usual, but they are both fit and healthy.'

'Then what is it that is troubling you?'

He looked startled.

'It's no use looking like that. I've known you since you were born, and I always know when there's something you're not telling me. When you threw a stone through the window of the greenhouse on your fifth birthday I knew straight away there was something worrying you. And when you took Blaze out of the stables without asking and brought him home lame. And when—'

'Enough!' he said, laughing, as he remembered his childhood worries.

'So why don't you tell us what is troubling you now?'

His mood darkened. He was not sure that he was ready to tell anyone about his troubles. He was about to deny that there was anything wrong when he hesitated. Maud had brought him up, and it would be impossible to fool her.

'Is it a young lady?' she asked, peering at him over her *pince-nez*.

'What makes you say that?' he prevaricated.

'Ah, good. So it is. And about time too. Now, who is she?'

Marcus bowed to the inevitable.

'Her name is Miss Wentworth,' he said.

'Wentworth.' She stopped her knitting and put her head on one side. 'I don't think I know any Wentworths. There was a Sir Toby Wentworth, I recall, but I did not know that he had any daughters.'

'She is not related to Sir Toby, or any other Wentworth, or at least none that you and Mother would have known. She is the daughter of a country doctor.'

'Ah. I see. So that is the problem. She is beneath you in rank. It does not bother you, of course, but it bothers her. She feels that you should marry someone from your own background, an earl's daughter, perhaps, or at least the daughter of a baron. Very proper. It shows great delicacy on her part.'

'No. That is not the problem.'

'No?' She looked at him enquiringly. 'Then what is? You love her, I take it?'

'I do. With all my heart and soul.'

'And she loves you?'

'Yes. She loves me as fiercely as I love her.'

'Then ask her again. She has refused you once, I collect, very properly, so now it is up to you to press your suit. You must tell her that the difference in your stations does not signify, that your mind is made up, and that you are determined to marry her. She needs only your reassurance, and she will be yours.' She put down her knitting. 'I am so glad. It is not good for you to live in the abbey on your own. You need a fresh start, a future, and your Miss Wentworth can give you one. '

'You talk as though the thing were possible,' he growled.

'Well, of course it is,' she returned. 'What is there to stop you? You are over age and she – she is also over age, I take it? You never did like simpering young chits.'

'Yes, she is over age. She is three-and-twenty.'

'Well then?'

'Well then?' he demanded. He pushed himself out of his chair and strode over to the window, looking out at the sea to calm himself. Then, turning round, he said, 'You know that it can never be.'

She looked genuinely surprised. 'I don't see why not. Unless—' A look of understanding crossed her face. 'Ah. I see. It is because of Esmerelda.'

'Yes.'

'Your Hilary, I take it, thinks she should be cared for in an asylum? She does not like the idea of a mad woman sharing the abbey with her?'

It was Marcus's turn to look surprised. 'No, of course not. She has no more love of asylums than I have. She thinks it is nonsensical to beat the mad, as well as cruel. She does not approve of what passes for "treatment" of those poor, tortured souls who, through no fault of their own, have lost their reason. Moreover, I would not love her if she wanted to put Esmerelda away.'

Maud put down her knitting. 'Then I can think of no other reason why you cannot marry her,' she said in exasperation. 'Really, Marcus, you did not used to be so contrary.'

He looked at her as though she was being wilfully blind. 'You know why I can't marry. You, of all people, must know that it can never happen.'

She abandoned all pretence of knitting. 'I don't know why not. And sit down, if you please. I cannot speak to you if you continue to tower over me like that.'

He sank into his chair and put his head in his hands. Then he sat up straight. 'I can never marry Hilary because I won't let her go through what my mother went through,' he said. The words were wrung out of him. 'I won't let her watch me slowly go mad.'

The logs crackled in the fire. They sounded unnaturally loud in the stillness.

Then Maud said, 'So that's it. I never imagined ... I never thought ... but of course, with what you know, it is not surprising. I should have seen it sooner. I knew that you seemed reluctant to marry, but I thought it was because you had not met anyone you loved. Which, of course, you had not. But now—'

The door opened and the maid entered the room with a tea tray.

She looked apprehensive, struck by the strange tension in the room. Instead of coming in, she lingered by the door.

'Thank you, Poll,' said Maud. 'Come in and put the tray down on the table.'

Poll did as she was bid, then bobbed a curtsy again before leaving the room.

'I think I should leave you now,' said Yvonne, with a significant glance at Maud. She stood up. 'It is very tiresome, but I have a headache. I hope you will excuse me. I cannot bring myself to take tea, and I will have a rest in my room instead.'

'A good idea,' said Maud. 'The fire is burning up nicely there. You will feel better after a nice lie down.'

Marcus was under no illusions regarding Yvonne's headache. He knew it was merely an excuse to enable her to leave the room, and if he could have made a similar excuse he would have done so. His nurse was evidently going to give him a lecture on not being able to see the future, or believing in Providence, or not abandoning hope, but he was in no mood for one of her homilies. But he couldn't avoid it, not without being rude to one of the few women he admired and respected. She had endured some terrible times at the abbey, when his father's madness had raged out of control, and through it all she had been a source of endless support to his mother, for which he would always be grateful.

Yvonne wrapped her shawl round her, then withdrew.

Marcus's nurse picked up the teapot. She poured out a cup of the amber liquid.

'I see now why you are so unhappy. You are in love with Hilary, but you will not marry her because you do not want to put her in danger, and you do not want her to have to watch you descend into madness.'

'Yes.' His voice was close to despair.

'In that case, I am going to do something I have never done before, and hope never to do again. I am going to betray a confidence.'

CHAPTER ELEVEN

$\mathcal{H}$ ilary was in the schoolroom, trying to interest the children in the globe, but her efforts were not meeting with success. Sara was staring into the middle distance, clearly engaged in a daydream, whilst Janet was sighing heavily and little Mary was engrossed in a fly which, almost dead with cold, was staggering round her desk.

'Who can tell me what this country is?' asked Hilary, pointing to England.

To her surprise and delight, Janet put up her hand.

'Yes, Janet?' she asked, encouraged by this sign of interest in her young charge.

'When is it time for tea?'

Hilary gave a sigh. 'Not yet. Now, can you tell me what this country is called?'

'America,' said Janet.

'No, it's not America, it's England. This is where we live, in England. See, here is America.' She twirled the globe. 'It is much bigger than England, and a different shape.'

'It's a different colour, too,' said Mary, taking an interest in the lesson as the fly staggered to a halt.

Hilary gave an inward sigh. Teaching the children was proving to be far more difficult than she had anticipated.

'Now I want you to draw me a picture of England on your slates,' she said, making the most of the fact that she had their attention. 'I want you to copy it carefully from the globe, looking particularly at the shape. Make sure your drawing is this shape as well.'

'I'm no good at drawing,' said Sara with a long-suffering air.

'Then this is your chance to practise,' replied Hilary.

She handed out the slates.

There was a sudden commotion outside the door, and Hannah rushed into the room. Her eyes were as round as saucers, and her whole demeanour spoke of her excitement.

'Oh, miss, you'll never guess, there's a lady as wants to see you downstairs.'

'A lady, Hannah?' asked Hilary in surprise.

'Yes, miss. A *real* lady, with a silk walking dress and a parasol, and dainty shoes, and smells just like lavender.'

'Do you know who she is?' asked Hilary.

'No, miss, I didn't catch her name, but she's in the parlour with Mrs Hampson, and the missus is like a dog with two tails. She's so pleased she got up this morning. There'll be no keeping her in bed after this! You're to go down at once, miss.'

'But the children . . .'

'Don't you mind them, miss. I'm to keep an eye on them for you while you're downstairs.'

Hilary shuddered to think of the chaos which would await her on her return, but she was nevertheless eager to discover who the lady could be.

'Very well, Hannah.' She turned to the children. 'Now, girls, I want you to behave yourselves for Hannah,' she admonished them, 'and I want to see your pictures of England when I return.'

Then, stopping only to check her appearance in the looking-glass on the landing, she went downstairs.

She could hear voices coming from the parlour. She went in.

There was Mrs Hampson, her eyes sparkling with delight, and there, sitting opposite her, was Mrs Palmer.

'Hilary! Would you believe it! Here is Mrs Palmer, kindly called to see how you do. She's been telling me all about how she met you at the abbey, and how she was delighted you could help Lord Carisbrooke with his library, and how she was just passing so she thought she'd call in to pay her respects.'

Hilary regarded Mrs Palmer with some surprise and not a little unease. It seemed strange that Mrs Palmer should decide to call on her.

'My dear Miss Wentworth, how good it is to see you again,' said Mrs Palmer, as though they were old friends. 'I have just been telling Mrs Hampson how much my daughter and I enjoyed your company at the abbey.'

'I'm not a bit surprised,' chimed in Mrs Hampson. 'Hilary's been an absolute blessing to Peter and me. She's been looking after the girls whilst I've been laid up in bed.'

She beamed at Hilary.

'If I could just have a word with Miss Wentworth alone?' asked Mrs Palmer.

Mrs Hampson looked put out at being asked to leave her own parlour, but it was only for a minute. Quickly rallying herself she said, 'Of course you can, I've got to see to the baby anyway.'

'Miss Wentworth, pray, do sit down,' said Mrs Palmer, once Mrs Hampson had left the room.

Hilary's eyebrows rose at Mrs Palmer's presumption in playing the part of the hostess, but nevertheless she took a seat, being curious as to what could have brought Mrs Palmer to the farmer's house.

'I expect you are wondering what I am doing here. I am aware that my daughter expressed herself rather thoughtlessly at the abbey, but I am sure you will forgive her. She is very young.'

Hilary privately thought that Miss Palmer was her equal in age, but said nothing, being interested to discover what Mrs Palmer had come to say.

'Lord Carisbrooke mentioned that you were looking for another position and by the greatest good chance I happened to hear of one which would suit you down to the ground,' said Mrs Palmer. 'As soon as I heard of it, I thought, *Miss Wentworth would enjoy that, and she'd give good service into the bargain. Why, it's made for her.* It offers a generous salary – far more than Mrs Hampson is able to pay you – and ample leave, besides being in the most beautiful location. Have you ever been to Scotland, Miss Wentworth?'

'No,' said Hilary.

'Then this is your chance to go. You will love the lochs and glens,' she said, in a voice which brooked no contradiction. 'It has inspired poets, and you will enjoy every minute of your time there.'

It was not difficult for Hilary to discover Mrs Palmer's motives for this sudden attack of concern on her behalf. Mrs Palmer, not knowing of Lord Carisbrooke's decision never to marry – perhaps not even knowing of the taint of madness in his blood, and believing that his sister was confined to her room through ill health, rather than insanity – had decided that Hilary was too near to the abbey for her liking and meant to send her to the far north. It was a dreadful piece of presumption on Mrs Palmer's part, but as Hilary did not want to remain in the vicinity of the abbey, or rather, she knew that she must not do it – for it was possible that if she did so her feelings would overcome her common sense – she was curious to learn more.

'And what is the position?' she asked.

'It is that of a secretary to a learned gentleman who is writing a book on architecture. He needs an intelligent person to help him compile his notes. Knowing your love of books, I realized it would be perfect for you.'

Hilary had to admit that it sounded perfect. If she must work, and must do it far away, then the post Mrs Hampson was outlining sounded ideal. Even so, she did not lose her caution. It was possible that Mrs Palmer had invented the position in order to remove her from the vicinity of the abbey.

'If the gentleman in question was to write and offer me the post, I feel sure I would be tempted to accept it,' said Hilary.

Mrs Palmer seemed unperturbed by this stipulation, leading Hilary to believe that it might, after all, be genuine.

'Of course. As long as I know you are interested in taking it up I will give him your name and your direction. Well, that is all I came to say.'

'Thank you,' said Hilary. 'It is very kind of you to take so much trouble.'

'It is no trouble,' said Mrs Palmer, rising. 'Now ring the bell, and send the maid for Mrs Hampson. I suppose I cannot go without bidding her farewell.'

Annoyed by Mrs Palmer's high-handed attitude, Hilary nevertheless rang the bell and a few minutes later, having bid her hostess adieu, Mrs Palmer went out to her waiting carriage.

So Mrs Palmer was still determined to remove her from the neighbourhood, thought Hilary. Her thoughts drifted back to her ordeal on the roof of the abbey. Had Mrs Palmer locked her out? It now seemed unlikely. Even so, she wished she had had an opportunity to find out whether the Lunds had accidentally locked the door behind her, trapping her on the roof, or whether they had known nothing about the incident. She had meant to ask Marcus, but events had moved so rapidly that she had not had a chance to do so. Still, where Mrs Palmer was concerned, she meant to be on her guard. She would make sure the position was genuine, not only by waiting for a letter from her supposed employer, but by writing to him independently before she set off for Scotland.

'What a surprise it was, to be sure, when I saw Mrs Palmer stepping out of her carriage,' said Mrs Hampson, eager to discuss the visit. 'She often goes by on her way to the abbey, with Miss Palmer beside her, but she has never stopped here before. You must have made quite an impression on her for her to take so much trouble. Did she have anything particular to say?'

Hilary did not take exception to Mrs Hampson's inquisitiveness. She was grateful to have found a safe haven, at least for the moment, and Mrs Hampson's interest in her affairs was a small price to pay for her present sanctuary.

'She came to tell me about a position she has heard of in Scotland that she thinks might suit me,' said Hilary.

'That is kind. I'm only sorry Mr Hampson and I can't keep you, you've been such a help to me already, looking after the older girls whilst I've been in bed, but what with the maid's wages and extending the house and now the new baby there's not a penny to spare. What sort of thing is it?'

Hilary told Mrs Hampson what she knew, and Mrs Hampson whiled away the next half-hour by speculating on the nature of the gentleman in question, whether he was old or young, married or unmarried, handsome or ugly. Hilary tried to rise several times, saying that she must return to the girls, but was met by a rejoinder of, 'Nonsense! They will be perfectly all right with Hannah.'

At last Mrs Hampson tired and, having been out of bed for the first time since the birth of her child, retired to her room, leaving Hilary to face the chaos in the schoolroom.

To her surprise, the girls were sitting and working industriously when she returned.

The reason for this was soon made apparent.

'If we're very good,' Mary informed her, the tip of her tongue protruding as she finished her picture, 'Hannah says there'll be cakes for tea.'

Marcus, seated in Maud's sitting-room, gave an inward sigh. Maud was going to betray a confidence, she had said, and that meant he must listen whilst she told him a story about the butcher, the baker, or the candlestick-maker.

He was used to such stories. Moralizing tales had formed a feature of his childhood, and many a brave child had been held up to him as a model when he had fallen out of the apple tree and broken his arm, or fallen from his pony. Then, too, there had been the stories about great scholars who had been held up as examples of the value of hard work, and the tales of saints that had been intended to lead to an improvement in his own behaviour.

Here, no doubt, was a story of courage in the face of adversity, or the benefits of endurance. It was the last thing he wanted to hear, but as he had a great deal of admiration for Maud he arranged his features into an interested expression and steeled himself to listen to whatever it was she had to say. After which, to please her, he would tell her that he had derived comfort from her words.

'Here.' She offered him a freshly poured cup of tea.

He took the cup.

'I am so sorry you have been made unhappy by the thought that you cannot marry Hilary, but that is not the case. You see, Marcus, there is no impediment to your marriage, because . . .'

He lifted the cup.

'. . . you are not Lord Carisbrooke's son.'

He paused with the cup just touching his bottom lip and turned uncomprehending eyes towards her. For a minute, he had thought she had said that he was not Lord Carisbrooke's son.

'So you see, there is no impediment to your marriage,' she said.

'I don't understand. Did you say – no, you can't have done – that I am not Lord Carisbrooke's son?' he said, lowering the cup.

'That's right,' said Maud placidly, taking up her knitting. 'I did.'

'But . . .' He put the cup back on its saucer. His hand had started to shake alarmingly, and he was suddenly afraid of dropping it.

'But . . . I don't understand.'

'It's really very simple,' she said, flicking the wool as she continued with her knitting. 'Lord Carisbrooke is not your father, and you are not his son.'

'But that would mean . . . no.' He shook his head firmly as he thought of what her words implied. 'My mother would never . . . I cannot believe it . . . Ah!' His expression cleared as he saw what lay behind her words, a desire to persuade him that he was not disbarred from marrying. 'I understand what you are doing. You are trying to convince me that it is all right for me to go ahead with my desire to marry Hilary.'

'Not at all,' she replied with asperity. 'I would not dream of lying to you in such a way, especially not over something so important. You should know me better than that.'

He wanted to believe her. Because if she was telling the truth, that would mean . . . An impossible hope began to dawn in his breast, but he refused to give into it until he knew for sure, because if his hopes were raised, only to be dashed again, it would be a bitter blow. One from which he might never recover.

'You must be wrong,' he said, shaking his head. 'My mother would never have betrayed my father.'

She sighed. 'I see I will have to tell you the whole story. I rather hoped you might believe me and ask nothing further, but I suppose it was not to be hoped for. I promised your mother I would never tell you, but she never foresaw this situation. If she had done, I am convinced she would have told you herself. But as she is no longer with us, I must make the decision for her and tell you instead.'

Marcus was not sure he wanted to hear more. If he did, he was afraid that he would discover his mother was not the woman he had thought she was. Because if he was illegitimate, then she must have deceived his father and had an affair. He could not believe it. His mother had been a wonderful woman, and never once in his childhood had he caught sight of another man at the abbey, which surely he would have done if she had been unfaithful.

But still, there was no doubt she had had some terrible things to endure, he thought with a frown. When his father's madness had driven her to distraction, perhaps she had taken solace in the arms of a normal man. She must have needed warmth and tenderness, love and kindness . . . things his poor, mad father was incapable of giving her.

Slowly his feelings began to change. It no longer seemed impossible that his mother might have been unfaithful. And if she had taken solace in the arms of another man, he found he could not blame her for it.

'So my mother had an affair,' he said.

'Certainly not,' returned Maud. 'She would never have done such a thing. The ties of marriage were sacred to her. That is why she nursed your father so lovingly through his insanity.'

'Then I must be Lord Carisbrooke's son!' he said in exasperation.

'No,' she said firmly. 'You are not.' She took up another ball of wool and tied it to the end of the one she had almost finished. 'You see, your mother was already with child when she married Lord Carisbrooke.'

'Then it is even worse. You are saying that she duped him into bringing up another man's child as his own,' he said, his voice hollow. He did not like what he was hearing.

'Not a bit of it,' she said, her needles clacking. 'What a low opinion you entertain of your mother.'

'You leave me no choice!' he declared. 'First of all you tell me that I am illegitimate, then that my mother was already with child when she married my . . . the man I thought was my father . . . tell me, what am I meant to think?'

'Yes. It is difficult to take in all at once,' she agreed. 'But you must not doubt your mother. She was the sweetest, gentlest, most loving woman that ever lived. But this, of course, you know. She never deceived Lord Carisbrooke – or, at least, what is more to the point, she never deceived his mother: for by that time Lord Carisbrooke was too far gone in madness to know what was happening, or even to care.'

Marcus put down his cup. 'Then you mean . . .' He thought. 'That she was a widow?'

'In a manner of speaking.'

'In a manner of speaking?' he demanded. Instead of growing clearer, her story was growing more obscure.

'I think I had better start at the beginning. I was your mother's nurse, as you know. I nursed her all through her childhood, and stayed on as her governess as she grew older. She was a lovely young woman.' Her knitting needles fell silent as she clearly became lost in a reverie. 'She was so pretty, and so full of life. It was no wonder your father – your real father – fell in love with her. He was a fine, upstanding young gentleman,' Maud explained. 'He was one of your mother's neighbours, the son of wealthy landowners. It was an excellent match, but it was more than that. Your mother and he were very much in love. They had grown up together, you see. They had played together as children, they had danced together at country balls, and no one was surprised when they fell in love.'

'Then how . . . ?'

'How did it happen that they never married? They would have done. Your father asked for your mother's hand, and it was gladly granted. Your grandparents, on both sides of the family, were in favour of the match. The wedding was arranged for the summer of 1780. The preparations were made, the banns were read. And then your father fell ill. It was only a minor indisposition, but the wedding could not go ahead and so it was postponed until the following month. Your father recovered, and everything went on as before. Until the outing.'

She fell silent.

'The outing?' Marcus prompted her.

She sighed. 'Yes. The outing.' She adjusted the knitted blanket, laying it more comfortably across her knee. 'It should have been a happy occasion. Your mother and father, together with their parents, were to go on a picnic to a local beauty spot, but in the morning your mother was very sick. It was taken to be a similar illness to the one endured by your father, and though unpleasant, there were no fears as to its outcome. At your mother's insistence, they went on the picnic without her. She never could bear to spoil anyone's pleasure. But as she continued to be sick she confided in me, telling me that she and your father had given in to their feelings just before the original date set for their wedding, and that she was now with child. I scolded her, of course, but there was no changing it, and besides, in another week she would be safely married. Or so we thought.'

Marcus began to have a presentiment.

'What happened?' he asked.

'There was an accident. The picnic spot was at the top of a steep hill. On the way back, one of the wheels came off the carriage. It overturned, killing everyone inside. When your mother was told she was beside herself with grief. In the space of one afternoon she had lost everyone she held dear: her fiancé, her parents, and her future parents-in-law, who were almost as close as her real parents to her. If not for the fact that she was with child, I believe she might have contemplated taking her own life, she was so stricken with grief. I pressed upon her the notion that she had something to live for, and though distraught, she at last began to rally.

'But then came another blow. Her father had speculated unwisely, and his death brought heavy debts to light. If he had lived, I have no doubt he would have righted himself, but he died at the worst possible moment, when his estate was worth almost nothing. Your mother had lost not only every one she loved, but her home and almost all her means of support as well.

'It was a bitter time. And to make matters worse, her condition was beginning to show. And so I brought her here, to Lyme. I had come here myself as a child, and been happy here, so I hoped the sea air would lift her spirits. It was then we met Lord Carisbrooke.'

Marcus let out a pent-up breath. The events she was unfolding were so unexpected that he had almost forgotten to breathe.

Outside, the light was growing dim.

'Or perhaps, I should say we met his mother,' continued Maud.

'How did it come about?' asked Marcus. Now that he had begun to come to terms with her revelation, he wanted to know everything he could about his mother, and the trials she had endured.

'Lord Carisbrooke was in Lyme, brought there by his mother, and for a similar reason. He was ill, and she had hoped he would benefit from the sea air.'

'He was mad?'

'He was. Of course, your mother and I did not know that at the time. We took a walk one morning. I can still remember it as though it was yesterday. It was a heavy day. The sky was grey, and the clouds were low. There was a keen wind blowing in from the sea. We were well wrapped up against the cold, and we walked along the beach. As we walked, the sun came out. We sat in a sheltered spot and talked over what was to be done. Your mother was hopeless, and I must confess I almost felt the same. We had next to no money, and when we had spent the tiny amount that was left to us we would be destitute. I spoke to her bracingly, but there was little I could do to relieve her gloom. We stopped speaking as a lady approached us, meaning to resume our conversation once she had gone by. But she did not go by. She said that she had overheard her conversation, and that if we would do her the honour of having dinner with her that evening she hoped she would be able to help us, and that in return we might be able to help her.'

She broke off, and looked at his cup. 'But you are not drinking your tea.'

'Tea! I hardly think this is a time for tea!' he exclaimed.

'Nonsense. It is exactly the time for tea. You have had a nasty shock.'

'What happened next?'

'Tea first,' she said, exactly as though he was still in the nursery. 'Then I will finish my tale.'

He gave a low growl, but nevertheless he took up his cup.

'And a biscuit,' she said.

He gave an exclamation of exasperation, but knew better than to argue with her. He had tried it many times in his childhood, and it had always failed.

He took a biscuit.

'I had the recipe from Mrs Wilson next door,' she said, as he ate it. 'She has several very good recipes, including an excellent one for ginger beer. Yvonne and I are quite taken with it.'

'It's very good,' said Marcus grudgingly. He knew she would not continue until he had expressed an opinion.

'I will tell Yvonne. She will be so pleased. She baked them herself.'

He dutifully drank his tea, then a second cup which she forced upon him.

Now,' he said, leaning back in his chair. 'Finish your tale.'

'Please,' she admonished him.

'I am not five years old any longer,' he protested.

'More's the pity,' she rebuked him. 'You had such lovely manners when you were five.'

'Hah! You would drive a saint to distraction! Finish your tale, if you please.'

'Very well.'

She pushed her *pince-nez* further up her nose, and then took up her story once more.

'Your mother and I did not know what to do. It seemed strange that an unknown lady should invite us to dinner. Had things been different, your mother would not have dreamt of accepting the invitation, but in the circumstances it seemed wise to do so, particularly as it meant we would eat well that day, at least. We were driven to such extremes at that time. We joined the unknown lady in the private parlour of an inn just outside Lyme and talked of pleasantries whilst the servants were bustling about, but once they had gone she began to speak.

'Her story was as tragic as your mother's. She had been married to the Earl of Carisbrooke – your supposed grandfather, the father of the man you thought was your sire – at a young age, and had been very happy with him. She had had three children. Two had died in infancy, leaving her with only one son. She had loved him dearly, and for a time all had been well. Then her husband had started to have what she described as "queer turns". His behaviour had been erratic. He had started to swear and throw things at the servants. But after each turn he had settled down again. Bit by bit, though, his turns had become more frequent, and each time they had been worse. They had lasted for longer and longer, and had started to include bouts of violence. Both she and her son had been badly hurt by him on several occasions. It was then she had discovered, during one of his periods of lucidity, that there was madness in his family, a taint he had thought he had escaped: only that belief had induced him to marry and father three children. But he had not escaped.

'She had naturally been shocked by his revelation, but she had cared for him as well as she could, until in a fit of madness he had thrown himself into the river and drowned.

'So she was left to bring up her son alone. For a time, she hoped the boy had escaped the family curse, but little by little the first signs began to appear. She kept him at the abbey, well looked after by a faithful couple of servants – you have them still, the Lunds – and from time to time she visited Lyme. The sea air made him calmer, and gave her some respite from her troubles. But she was sick at heart. She was going to lose her son, and after that she would have no one. She had been feeling desperate, she told us, when she had gone for a walk that morning. She had been longing for grandchildren to ease her loneliness and brighten her old age, but she could not allow an unsuspecting young woman to marry her son. She herself had been through agonies watching her husband descend into madness, and she would not inflict that on any other woman. And so she had seen nothing ahead for her but the sorrow of her son's death and a lonely old age. And then she had heard your mother and I talking and an idea had come to her. If your mother agreed to marry her son, your mother would have a home and would be free from want. Moreover, your mother would have a father for her child and would be able to give it the protection of his name. And your grandmother – I call her your grandmother still, for although she was never related to you by blood, she loved you as truly as if she was your real grandmother – would have a child at the abbey, someone to bring sunshine and laughter into her old age. She would have the joy of watching a "grandchild" grow, and she would be able to relax, safe in the knowledge that it would not be tainted by madness.'

Marcus sat back, trying to digest everything he had heard. There had not been only one tragedy in the past, but two. His grandmother, or at least the woman he had called his grandmother, losing her husband and then her son to madness; and his mother, losing everything in one terrible accident. And yet out of both tragedies something good had come. His mother had found a safe haven, and his grandmother had found a family to love.

'Then I am truly not Lord Carisbrooke's son.'

At last he believed it. With the knowledge came a huge sense of relief. He felt suddenly lighter, as the enormous burden he had carried on his shoulders all his life lifted and floated away.

He gave a deep sigh.

He would not go mad.

But then his euphoria began to dissipate. Maud's story had told him much, but there were still many things he wanted to know.

'What I don't understand,' he said at last, 'is how my mother came by Esmerelda.'

'Ah, yes. Esmerelda.' Maud's hands stilled. 'That was a dark day. Or perhaps I should say, a dark night.'

Marcus paled. He began to have an understanding of what was about to come.

'Your father – that is to say, Lord Carisbrooke – was looked after by Lund, but one night Lund was taken ill. With the cunning that was a hallmark of his madness, Lord Carisbrooke took the key of his room from Lund's waistcoat and escaped. He found your mother in her bedroom.' She paused. 'Esmerelda was the result.'

Marcus put his head in his hands.

'My poor mother.'

She spoke consolingly. 'Your mother never blamed him for it, and neither should you. It was not the cruel act of a rational man, but the unthinking instinct of a poor, sad creature, who was too far gone in madness to know what he was doing. Besides, your mother loved your sister. She even hoped, for a time, that Esmerelda had escaped the family curse. But it was not to be.'

Outside the window, afternoon was giving way to evening. Daylight was fading, and it was almost dark.

Maud laid aside her knitting.

Crossing to the mantelpiece, she lit the candles in the candelabras. Her old hands shook slightly as she did so.

Marcus watched her simple actions lovingly. Amidst so much that was changing, she was a familiar sight. He found it soothing to watch her, as he had watched her many times before, going about her simple routine. She lit the candles and blew out the taper, putting it back in its holder at the side of the mantelpiece. Then she bent down to tend to the fire. She took the poker from its place on the hearth and riddled the glowing coals, making them shift and spark. Then she returned the poker to its stand and took up the tongs. Carefully lifting a lump of coal out of the scuttle she placed it over the glowing coals, arranging another six lumps before deciding that it was enough. The red glow of the burning coals could still be seen, but the new ones placed on top of them were beginning to catch light, ensuring that the fire would not go out.

'So now you know,' she said. She straightened up again.

'Yes. Now I know.'

He sat quietly, digesting all he had heard.

He was not Lord Carisbrooke's son, and it had changed everything. But before he could allow himself to rejoice he must voice the one thought that still disturbed him. 'If I am not Lord Carisbrooke's son, then I am not entitled to my inheritance,' he said. 'I have no claim on the fortune, the title or the abbey.'

Maud resumed her seat.

'You certainly have. The fortune was your grandmother's, and not your grandfather's. She had a right to leave it to whomever she wanted, and she chose to leave it to you.'

'Then Laurence has no claim on it,' said Marcus.

'None at all. Besides, even if he did, he would not need it. Laurence has a fortune of his own.'

Marcus thought of the large fortune Laurence's mother had left him, and was content on that score.

'But the title . . .' he said.

'Laurence has never expressed any interest in it, indeed I have heard him describe titles as vulgar. And he would not want the abbey. He regards it as a decrepit pile,' she said with a sigh.

Marcus nodded. He had heard Laurence make disparaging remarks about the abbey on many occasions.

Now that his questions had been answered, he sat quietly, thinking over everything he had heard. His mother's sad story, his grandmother's tragic tale, his own origins and the details surrounding Esmerelda's birth.

As he pondered the revelations, he was at last able to give way to the joy he had felt growing inside him ever since he had discovered that he was not Lord Carisbrooke's son. Burgeoning inside him was a happiness he had thought he would never be able to feel, as the full meaning of the revelations was made clear.

His face broke into a smile. He had a future ahead of him, one that was bright and full of promise. He could marry Hilary. He could take her into his arms and love her and cherish her for the rest of his life.

He stood up. 'I have to go.'

'Yes, my dear,' said Maud with a smile.

'I never thought it possible that I could be so happy! There seemed to be no way of escaping my terrible destiny, and now everything has changed.'

The door opened. Yvonne stood there.

'May I come in?

Maud said, 'You are just in time. Marcus is leaving us.'

'Ah. Then you have told him,' Yvonne said to her sister.

'Indeed I have.'

'And about time, too.' She turned to Marcus. 'I have often felt Maud should tell you the truth, but she never saw the need. Until now.'

'I could not let Marcus throw away his chance of happiness,' said Maud.

'No, indeed. I am so glad you are to marry, Marcus. A wife will remove the haunted look from your eyes. You have had much to bear.'

'You will wait until morning?' asked Maud.

Marcus glanced out of the window. Night had fallen, but he was eager to be on his way. 'No. I have a long journey before me. I want to make a start.'

'Then we will wish you God speed,' said Maud. 'And mind you bring Hilary to visit us,' she added with a smile.

'I will,' he promised her. 'Just as soon as I've made her my wife.'

CHAPTER TWELVE

$\mathcal{M}$arcus had never accomplished the return journey from Lyme so quickly. He spared neither his coachman nor his horses, and a few days after leaving Maud's home he was entering his own neighbourhood once again.

'The Hampson farmhouse,' he called out of the window to his coachman. 'And stop when you get there.'

The coach pulled up in front of the neat farmhouse. Marcus opened the door before it had fully stopped and, without waiting for the step to be let down, he leapt out. His impatience had been growing throughout the journey, and now that he was within reach of Hilary it knew no bounds. Striding up the path, the hem of his great-coat flying, he rapped at the door.

It seemed a lifetime before Hannah answered it, though it was only a few minutes.

'I'm here to see Miss Wentworth,' he growled as he strode into the house. 'Be so good as to bring her to me.'

'Yes, your lordship,' said Hannah, clearly overawed by the sheer size of him, and by the knowledge that she had an earl in the house. 'Only she's—'

'Who is it, Hannah?' came Mrs Hampson's voice as she came into the kitchen, eager to greet her guest. 'I – oh!'

She appeared to be dumbfounded at the sight of Lord

Carisbrooke in her kitchen! For once the worthy woman was speechless.

'My lord!' she gasped at last.

'I have come to see Miss Wentworth,' he said, trying to conceal his impatience and belatedly remembering to ask about Mrs Hampson's health, the health of her husband and children, and of her new baby.

'Never better, thank you, your lordship, the whole family, and the baby is thriving. We are so grateful to Hilary. She's been such a help.'

'Bring her to me, if you please,' he said, tapping his hand against the side of his leg.

'Of course, your lordship. Hannah, run out and get Miss Wentworth.'

'Out?' Marcus queried.

'She's taken the children into the woods,' Mrs Hampson explained. 'They were getting rather fractious, though never better children drew breath, I do assure your lordship, and she took them out for a nature walk. They're to collect leaves,' she explained helpfully.

Marcus almost exploded. Here he was, ready to sweep Hilary into his arms, and she was not to be found!

He was almost tempted to stride into the woods after her, but he would not be able to give way to his feelings once he found her if she was indeed with the children. He could hardly sweep her into his arms and cover her mouth, her face and her hair with his kisses, whilst the little girls looked on.

'How long has she been gone?' he demanded.

'Not long,' said Mrs Hampson.

He cursed under his breath. If she had not been gone long, then she would not be back for some time.

A moment's reflection showed him that perhaps this was no bad thing. He was not expected at the abbey, for he had travelled so quickly that he had not thought to send word ahead, and the fires would be banked down. When he was away the Lunds retreated to the kitchen and the fires in the main rooms were kept very low to prevent a deep chill from penetrating the stone walls, but nothing more. If he had found Hilary at home he would have carried her back to the abbey at once but she would have found a cold set of rooms and no dinner waiting for her. If he went on ahead these evils could be cured.

'Bring me paper, if you please,' he said to Hannah, 'and a quill.'

'Won't you come into the parlour?' asked Mrs Hampson.

'Yes. Thank you.' He gave an apologetic growl. 'I should not be giving your servant orders.'

'Pray don't mention it. I'm sure Hannah doesn't mind any more than I do,' said Mrs Hampson, agog to know what he wanted to write.

'Ooh no,' said Hannah.

'You are very good,' he said with a bow.

Mrs Hampson led him through to the parlour, where she supplied him with a quill and paper.

He sat down at the table, dwarfing it with his immense size.

'Do you have sealing wax?' he asked.

'No, my lord, there's not a stick in the house,' said Mrs Hampson.

Marcus nodded. He had not expected it. Still, it meant he must keep his note to Hilary brief, for he knew that Mrs Hampson would not be able to resist looking at the message.

My dear Miss Wentworth, he wrote, *Pray join me at the abbey as soon as you are able to do so.*

He signed it with a simple C.

'Give this to Miss Wentworth as soon as she returns, if you please,' he said.

'Yes, my lord. Very good, my lord. Will you stay for tea?'

'That is very kind of you, but I'm afraid I cannot stay,' he said. 'I must return to the abbey.'

'I'll see Hilary gets this just as soon as she gets in.'

'Thank you.'

Pausing only to compliment her on the neatness of her house, and the orderliness of her farmyard, Marcus strode out to the waiting carriage and was once more on his way.

How long would it be before he could reasonably expect Hilary? he wondered, glancing at his fob watch. It was two o'clock now. Perhaps by three . . . .

The coach passed through the abbey gates.

His eyes swept over the weed-infested drive and the tangled shrubbery beyond. All this will soon be changed, he thought. Now that he had a future, he was eager to restore the abbey to its former glory, making it a suitable abode for his future wife – and, God willing, his future children.

The coach rolled to a halt outside the door.

He jumped out, and strode up the steps, pulling the bell rope so hard it nearly broke.

He waited impatiently for Lund to open the door . . . and waited . . . and waited . . . .

Perhaps Lund, not expecting him, was in the attic, or otherwise out of hearing of the bell.

He turned the iron ring in the hope that the door was not barred and had a feeling of satisfaction as it opened. Good.

He went in.

As he had suspected, the fire in the hall had been allowed to die down, so that it was little more than glowing embers.

He crossed the hall and went into the drawing-room. There was still no sign of Lund. He was just about to pull the bell rope that hung beside the fireplace when his eyes stopped, arrested by an unusual sight. The secret door to the side of it was ajar.

Why was the secret passage open? And who had opened it?

Lund?

Possibly. But why should he do so?

Mrs Lund?

She used the passage from time to time as a short cut through the abbey, it was true, but she would have closed the door behind her.

Esmerelda . . . ?

His heart misgave him. If Esmerelda had escaped again . . .

Even as he thought it, he strode towards the passage.

If Esmerelda had escaped, that would explain Lund's absence, for the trusted servant would be looking for her. But how could she have done so? The windows of the cottage were barred, and the door bolted. Nevertheless, someone had opened the secret door.

Pausing only to take up a candelabra and light the candles from the glowing embers of the fire, Marcus went into the secret passage. It had been a favourite playground of Esmerelda's when they had been children. It enclosed a secret room which had been used for hiding priests in bygone days, and which, in the days of their childhood, had housed a table and chairs. They had spent many happy hours there, running into the secret passage in the drawing-room and climbing the secret stair to emerge into the small bedroom behind the tapestry, or taking fruit and tarts into the secret room and having an impromptu picnic. If she had escaped, led on by hazy memories, Esmerelda might well have run in there to play.

'Esmerelda!' called Marcus, holding the candelabra aloft as he went further into the passageway. 'Esmerel—'

His voice stopped in shock.

His heart lurched. And then there was a sickening thud.

Hilary's afternoon was passing pleasantly. The wet spell having given way to a period of dry, settled weather, she had decided to take the children outside for a few hours so that they could run about in the fresh air. Her idea was being rewarded by their improved behaviour. Away from the confines of the farmhouse the children no longer argued with each other, but were content to run about and play. After they had run off their surplus energy, Hilary had set them the task of finding as many different kinds of leaves as they could. They ran hither and thither, picking up the brown, yellow and orange leaves that carpeted the woodland floor.

Hilary sat on a fallen log, enjoying the scene. The sky was blue and the branches of the trees formed a delicate tracery against it. The sun was surprisingly strong for the time of year, and was warming her cheek. If not for the fact that she was missing Marcus she would have been happy.

Where was he now? she wondered. Was he in Lyme, walking by the sea? Or talking to his mother's old nurse? Was he happier, now that he was away from the abbey? She hoped so. But for her, there had been no alleviation of her low spirits. She felt her parting from Marcus as deeply as she had done when she had left the abbey. She felt as though she had lost the vital spark of herself. It was as though she was a sleepwalker, and try as she might, she could not shake off her gloom.

Her thoughts were broken into by Sara, who brought her some leaves to identify. Giving her attention to the little girl, she told her what all the leaves were, identifying the last two as horse chestnuts.

'But they're not the same,' protested Sara, holding them up. 'This one has five bits and this one has only three.'

'That's because this one is damaged,' explained Hilary.

She helped Janet identify the leaves she had found, then turned her attention to Mary, who had fallen over a tree root when chasing a squirrel, and had grazed her knee.

At last, tired but happy, and clutching their collections of leaves, Hilary took the children back to the farmhouse, knowing they would sleep well that night.

As they approached the house, the door flew open and Mrs Hampson was revealed.

Hilary was startled. It was not Mrs Hampson's habit to open the door to her, and she wondered whether anything could be wrong.

But Mrs Hampson's first words reassured her.

'Such news! Such *good* news!' crowed Mrs Hampson.

Hilary had hardly set foot in the door when Mrs Hampson began.

'You will never guess who's been here?'

Hilary felt a sinking sensation. Surely Mrs Palmer had not visited her again?

'Lord Carisbrooke! That's who!'

Hilary's heart began to beat more quickly.

Marcus? Here? At the farmhouse?

'But surely he is in Lyme . . . ?'

'Not any more,' said Mrs Hampson triumphantly. 'He's back. Go upstairs, girls, and take off your coats,' she said, turning to the children. 'Hannah will go with you. And make sure you wash your hands,' she admonished them.

The girls groaned, but they were so tired that they only did so half-heartedly. They followed Hannah upstairs.

Hilary was glad of the few minutes Mrs Hampson's interest in the children had given her, as it had allowed her to school her thoughts, so that no trace of consciousness remained. She felt she could now talk about Marcus without betraying her feelings by any sudden start or flush.

'I knew you would be surprised,' said Mrs Hampson. 'Lord Carisbrooke has been here this very afternoon! But we can't stand here talking in the kitchen. Come into the parlour.'

They went through into the parlour, where Mrs Hampson handed Hilary Marcus's letter.

Hilary took it with trembling fingers. The letter would no doubt be nothing but a formal note, telling her that he had managed to find her a well-paid post. Still, it would be in his own hand, and she longed to see it.

'What do you think?' asked Mrs Hampson. 'He didn't even go back to the abbey first, but came straight from Lyme just to see you. Hannah asked his coachman. But I must stop talking and let you read. It says you're to go to the abbey as soon as you can,' she went on, as Hilary perused the brief note. 'No doubt he's found you a position. I knew he would. He's always been so helpful. He's a wonderful landlord, that's what my Peter says. Perhaps he heard of something when he went to Lyme. I wonder what kind of position it is . . . .'

Hilary scarcely heard her as she rattled on. Her one thought was that Marcus wanted to see her. True, it would be about a position, and true, that position would in all likelihood remove her from his neighbourhood for ever, but she could not stop her heart beating faster. She would see Marcus again . . . .

Was it wise to go to the abbey? she asked herself.

Assuredly not, came the reply.

But she chose not to listen, for at that moment wisdom was unimportant to her. What mattered was that she would see Marcus one more time; hear his voice; be in his company; feel him near.

'You will be wanting to set off straight away,' said Mrs Hampson. 'And you will be needing the trap. Will you be back for dinner, do you think, or will you be eating at the abbey?'

'I don't know,' said Hilary. 'If I am not back in time, pray start without me.'

'Now what about the trap. Will you keep it at the abbey?'

'No.' Hilary shook her head. 'I will return it once I have arrived. I am sure Lord Carisbrooke will arrange for me to be brought safely back to the farmhouse.'

'And so am I, for never a better man lived, and this is the proof of it, that he's found you a position so soon.'

They went out into the farmyard, where Tom, one of the farmhands was working.

'Fetch the trap, Tom,' said Mrs Hampson. 'Miss Wentworth is going to the abbey.'

Tom put down his pitchfork and wiped his hands on his breeches, then departed.

Mrs Hampson continued to talk as Tom brought the trap, then Tom helped Hilary up beside him and they were off.

She should focus her thoughts on her prospective position, Hilary knew, but they would not do her bidding, and instead of asking herself whether the position was that of a governess or companion, she found herself wondering how Marcus would look, what he would say, and whether he would be filled with a longing to kiss her, as she was filled with a longing to kiss him.

She tried to turn her thoughts aside as the trap made its way along the country lanes to the abbey, but they kept returning to Marcus. She had hoped she would be able to quell her feelings for him, but she was perturbed to find they were as strong as ever.

At last they reached the abbey. How different it looked, compared to the first time she had approached it. Then it had seemed a gloomy pile, seen in the dismal light of a stormy day. Now, with the sun shining, it seemed less oppressive. In fact, if not for its tragic secret, it would almost have seemed welcoming.

'Thank you, Tom,' she said, as he handed her out of the trap.

He climbed back into it and geed up the horse, then drove away down the drive.

Hilary climbed the shallow steps that led to the massive door. With beating heart she pulled the rope and heard the bell clanging through the house.

As she waited for Lund to answer it, she reflected that it was not only the appearance of the abbey that had changed. She, too, had changed. She was no longer the same young woman who had arrived there not long ago.

Lund was slow in answering the door. It gave her time to adjust her reticule and smooth her pelisse. But the minutes passed, and still Lund did not come. She rang the bell again. Again there was no reply.

She tried the door, and it opened. She went in.

An eerie stillness greeted her. She was suddenly apprehensive.

But that was ridiculous, she told herself. There was no reason to be apprehensive. Marcus must be in the abbey somewhere. There was nothing to fear.

She crossed the hall. With no sign of Caesar and the fire banked down it seemed cold and empty. She pulled her pelisse more closely about her and made her way to Marcus's study. The door was open. She went in, hoping to find him, but there was no sign of him. She stood for a minute, and then decided to go to the library, but it, too, was deserted.

The abbey's emptiness was beginning to prey on her nerves. Where was Marcus? And where was Lund?

Rallying herself, she decided that in all probability Marcus had taken Caesar for a walk and that Lund was in some far flung corner of the abbey where he could not hear the bell. She decided to wait for Marcus in the drawing-room.

Once in the drawing-room, she went over to the fireplace and warmed her hands at the banked-down fire. As she did so she noticed that there were drips of wax on the floor, next to the fireplace. They must have been dropped by Marcus's candle on the day he had dragged Esmerelda, spitting and struggling, into the secret passage, she reflected. She would have thought that Mrs Lund would have cleaned them up by now, for the housekeeper usually managed to keep the main rooms clean and tidy, even if she did not manage to maintain the rest of the abbey.

Hilary bent down, meaning to scrape the wax from the floor, but to her surprise she discovered that it was still soft. She frowned. It must have been dropped recently. She stood up, rubbing it between her thumb and forefinger. As she did so, she looked at the secret door.

Had Marcus used the secret passage that afternoon? And had he somehow been shut in? No. It wasn't possible. The door had an opening mechanism on the inside, as well as on the outside.

But what if he had been attacked by Esmerelda? What if he was unable to open the door because he was hurt?

Worried by the thought, Hilary took a candle from the silver candlestick on the console table, thrust it into the fire and waited until the wick caught light. Then, replacing it in the candlestick, she pulled down the wall sconce and opened the passage. It did not look inviting. It was dark and dusty. She shivered. She had never liked the dark. But telling herself not to be so lily-livered, and reminding herself that Marcus might need her, she went in.

It was dank in the passage, and the air was stale. She grimaced. But still she went further in, shivering as the cold, damp atmosphere closed around her.

She stood still for a minute, giving her eyes time to adjust to the gloomy light, then began to make out the shape of the passage. It was no more than four feet wide and seven feet high. Cobwebs hung from the ceiling. They were grey and ghostly in the flickering candle-light. The floor was covered with a thick layer of dust. On the wall to her left was a shelf running the length of the passageway. Candlesticks placed at regular intervals showed that it had been once used to provide light, but the stumps of candles, encrusted with solidified wax drippings, were not lit.

If Marcus was in the passage, then would he not have lit them? she asked herself. Not if he had been intending to do no more than go through, she realized.

She took a deep breath and went on. The floor was uneven, being made of earth, and she moved cautiously, not wanting to risk a fall. Fortunately, her curiosity had led her to study the plans of the abbey she had found in the library when she had been staying there, and she knew the layout of the passage. Ahead of her there would be a side passage, which would open to her left and lead to a secret chamber used for hiding priests in centuries gone by. If she ignored it she would soon reach the spiral staircase which led to the room behind the tapestry.

She glanced over her shoulder for reassurance. Behind her, she could still see a glimmer of light from the open door. Even so, she was glad of her candle, and put her hand round it to protect the flickering flame.

Slowly she progressed. The daylight from the doorway became dimmer, until at last it disappeared and she was left with nothing but the candlelight to guide her.

She went on . . . and then let out a cry of fright. Something had brushed her face! For one heart-stopping moment her imagination took flight, and she imagined ghosts and ghouls and other monsters from the novels she had read. But when she hit out at it she found herself laughing, for it was nothing but a cobweb.

She continued on her way. At last she came to the turning to the secret chamber. She was just wondering whether she should follow it, or whether she should continue towards the stairs, when she felt the hairs stand up on the back of her neck. There was a noise . . . coming from the room!

M . . . Marcus?

She tried to say the name, but nothing came out.

It must be Marcus, she told herself. But her heart began to thud in her chest.

The noise came again, a scraping noise.

She tried hard not to think of all the ghostly things it could be, but the darkness frightened her.

Then there came a rushing of air and a pair of strong hands grabbed her in an iron grip.

'No!' She almost dropped her candle in her terror and fought to break free.

'Hilary!'

The voice was startled.

'Marcus!' This time she had no difficulty in saying his name. 'Oh, Marcus,' she gasped in relief as she turned to face him. 'I thought . . . but never mind what I thought. It is you.'

And it was. It was Marcus, with his massive frame and his grizzled hair, his deep-set eyes and his jutting brow.

His face softened. 'It is,' he said.

His voice was warm and tender, and made her melt inside.

And then – she did not know how it happened, but between him reaching out for her in order to soothe her, and her swaying against him in the aftermath of her fear, she found herself in his arms.

Their embrace was awkward, for they were both clutching their candlesticks, but still it felt wonderful.

Until Hilary remembered that she was not meant to be in his arms.

Reluctantly, she pulled away, then lifted her candle so that she could see his face more clearly. In the flickering light, it was altered. There were dark shadows at the side of his face and yellow highlights on his nose, forehead and cheeks. And yet it was still his face, and she found it wonderfully comforting.

Even better, she saw that he was smiling.

She had rarely seen him smile. His troubles had cast a darkness over his countenance, but now his face was softened by the unfamiliar expression.

'My love . . .' he began.

My love. The words were wonderful to Hilary's ears. But they were also perilous. Sensing the danger, she took a step backwards and ignored his words.

'I came in here hoping to find you, but when I did so I thought . . . never mind what I thought,' she said.

'You thought I was a ghost?'

His voice was warm and teasing. There was something so reassuring about his tone that she smiled.

'Yes,' she admitted.

'There are no ghosts in here, my darling.'

Again, a term of endearment. It sent shivers down her spine. It was wonderful to hear him calling her *love* and *darling*, but she must not let him. Especially not here, away from other people, when they were trapped together in a confined space. If she gave in to her emotions, as he had given in to his, there would be no stopping, for her feelings were burning inside her even now, growing and swelling and threatening to overflow the walls she had built around them. So she must stop him speaking to her in such a way. But it was hard for her to be strong. She wanted to match his loving words with loving words of her own. She wanted to reach out and touch him; stroke his grizzled hair; trace the con tours of his face with her fingers; let them linger on his lips.

But she must not do it.

She must push him away from her, not with her hands but with her words. She must make them formal. Aloof.

Putting all her effort into controlling her wayward emotions, which even now cried out to be in his arms, she said, 'What are you doing in here?'

Her voice had come out as calmly as she had wished. It was level, and betrayed not even a hint of what she felt.

But he did not respond to her tone. Instead of joining her in formality, his eyes traced her face in the most intimate way, and she felt her pulse begin to race.

She must not give into temptation.

She must not.

'Were you . . . were you looking for Esmerelda?' she asked, steadying her voice and determinedly speaking of practical matters.

Her words had the desired effect. His eyes stopped following the contours of her cheek and lips.

'Yes.'

She gave a sigh of relief. Her choice of conversation was doing what she hoped. It was breaking the intimate moment, and restoring a more neutral tone.

'Has she escaped again?'

In the candlelight she saw him frown. 'I'm not sure. When I returned to the abbey, Lund did not answer the door. I went into the drawing-room and found the secret passage was ajar. Fearing that Esmerelda had escaped and that she had decided to play in the secret chamber, I came in to search for her.'

'But you did not find her?'

'No.'

'Then, if she is not here, I suggest we leave,' said Hilary with a shiver.

'You're cold,' he said.

He stretched out his hand and cupped her cheek. His touch was warm and gentle. It was also stimulating. How she longed to kiss the fingers that hovered near her mouth! But she knew she must not do it. To do so would reawaken feelings that were better left undisturbed.

'It's nothing. I don't like the dark,' she said, turning her head away.

'Then we will go at once.' He took her hand. 'Now that you're here, the door must be open again.'

'Again?' she queried, trying to take her mind from the wonderful feeling of his large fingers wrapped round her tiny hand.

'It slammed shut behind me when I first ventured in,' he explained. 'I was just calling for Esmerelda when the daylight suddenly disappeared and there was a sickening thud. I was shut in.'

Hilary shuddered. 'How dreadful. How did it happen?'

'I'm not sure. Either a gust of wind must have blown it shut, or Esmerelda must have shut it deliberately. We will have to be careful when we leave the passage. She might be waiting for us outside.'

The thought was not a pleasant one. Esmerelda was unpre-dictable; at times charming, at times violent. To take her mind from the thought of what might be waiting for them outside the passage, Hilary said, 'But why did you remain here? Why did you not use the lever to open the door?'

'It's broken,' he said. 'Esmerelda must have kicked it in her strug-gle when I brought her through here to escape from the Palmers.'

He led her back along the narrow passage. The rectangle of daylight from the open door began to grow larger as they approached it.

But just as they reached it, it slammed shut with a thud.

Hilary's heart jumped into her mouth.

'Hell's teeth!' cursed Marcus. 'This is exactly what happened to me.'

Reminding herself that there was nothing to worry about, Hilary forced her pulse to calm and said, 'We will just have to get out at the other end.'

Marcus came to a halt. 'We can't.'

Hilary stopped behind him.

In the narrowness of the passage, he turned to face her.

'The door is blocked,' he explained. 'Mrs Lund had been cleaning the room. It was occupied by Esmerelda when we had the thunder-storm, as you know. Esmerelda does not like storms, they frighten her, and in her fear she threw her food and drink over the walls. Some of it went behind the wardrobe, and Mrs Lund asked me to move it so that she could clean behind it. It is still blocking the secret door.'

'And the door opens outwards?' asked Hilary in a small voice.

'It does.'

'Then we are trapped.' Her shoulders slumped.

'Don't worry,' he said tenderly. 'It won't be for long. If Esmerelda has escaped, then Lund and Mrs Lund will be searching for her. As soon as they find her they will know what she has done, for she will brag about her cleverness. Then they will let us out.'

'But that could take hours,' said Hilary, her voice sinking.

In response to her despondent tone, his strong fingers stroked her palm. The feel of them was comforting and reassuring. It was also enlivening. Even here, in a dark passage festooned with cobwebs and thick with dust, his fingers set her quivering, driving out fear and hopelessness, dismissing everything but the need to be touched by him and to touch him in return.

'The time will pass quickly,' he said throatily. 'There is so much I have to tell you.' His eyes sought her own. 'I never thought it would be possible for me to do this with any sense of honour, but now at last I can give in to my desires.'

His free arm encircled her and drew her close.

'Hilary, you know I love you,' he said.

His mouth hovered mere inches from her own.

She was torn between a need to give in to her innermost desires, and a feeling that she should pull away, but she found it impossible to resist. Besides, he had said that he could kiss her with honour, and although she did not know how that could be, she knew he would not have lied about such a thing.

And then the time for thought was gone. He took her candlestick from her and set it on a shelf behind them, putting his own beside it, then his mouth closed over her own.

The kiss sent shivers down her spine. She twined her arms around his neck, holding him close. The feel of his large body next to her own was intoxicating, and the sensation of his mouth moving over hers was exhilarating. His lips transported her to a different world, one of heat and passion, longing and desire. Her own parted instinctively, welcoming the intimate contact, and as she felt the touch of his tongue she was lost to all else.

As he deepened the kiss he held her closer and closer still. His hands slid downwards, pressing her more firmly against him so that there was no space between them, and she tightened her own embrace in response.

'Hilary,' he murmured, as his mouth left hers and he nuzzled her ear, her neck and her hair. 'At last you can be mine.'

He pulled away from her, holding her face in his hands, and his eyes wandered over her, drinking her in.

'Every part of you is dear to me,' he said. 'Your brow' – he kissed it – 'your nose' – he kissed it – 'your eyelids' – he kissed them – 'your mouth.' And once again, he was pulling her towards him, drowning her in a sea of wonderful sensations and leaving her breathless and weak.

'This is not how I imagined it would be, when I could finally kiss you without threatening either your honour or your happiness,' he said, as at last he let her go. 'I did not think it would be in a dusty passage full of cobwebs, lit only by a few candles flickering in the darkness.'

Emerging from her dream-like state, Hilary straightened her bonnet, which had fallen off the back of her head. 'Nor I,' she whispered.

'Ah. So you have imagined it?' he asked, with a growl of satisfaction.

She wished she could deny it, but she could not. Her unruly thoughts had kept reminding her of the times he had taken her in his arms and kissed her, and her dreams had been even worse. They had tormented her every night in her sleep. In them, Marcus had come to her. He had kissed her eyes, her throat and her lips, and had not stopped there. He had kissed and caressed every inch of her . . . .

'You will make me blush,' she said, feeling hot and embarrassed, and thanking Providence he could not read her thoughts.

'I certainly hope so,' he returned.

The glance that accompanied his words was so smouldering that she had the sudden wonderful feeling that his dreams had equalled hers.

He cupped the back of her head. His head tilted, and she knew he was going to kiss her again. She longed for him to do it, but having been overwhelmed by him once, she was determined not to be over-whelmed again. At least not until she knew what his enigmatic words had meant.

'You said you could kiss me with honour,' she reminded him, taking a small step back, which was all the confines of the passage would allow. 'What has changed?'

'Everything. Hilary, there is so much I have to tell you. I learnt a great deal when I went to Lyme, and all of it wonderful and unexpected. But I will not talk of it here. The passage is dank and confined. There is a small chamber leading off to one side of it, a little further on. It has a table and a few chairs, and whilst not comfortable, it is better than where we are.'

Hilary nodded.

He picked up his candelabra and handed her her own single candlestick. Then he led her back along the narrow passage. Turning to the left, he followed an even narrower tunnel until it gave on to a small room.

Hilary held her candle aloft as she entered it. The room was some eight feet square, and her dim light revealed four upright chairs, an armchair and a low table. All were covered in dust.

'Esmerelda and I used to play here when we were children. It was one of our favourite places. We have had many a game in this very room. It was much cleaner then, of course. The abbey used to have a full complement of servants, before my fath— Lord Carisbrooke's madness turned to violence and drove them away. The room was always swept and dusted along with the rest of the house.'

'I can see why you liked to play here,' said Hilary, looking round.

Dim though the light was, it was enough to reach into the corners of the small chamber. 'It's a perfect den for children. It's small and cosy and hidden away from the rest of the abbey.'

He set his candlestick down on the table then took out a large handkerchief and used it to dust one of the chairs.

Setting her candle on the table beside Marcus's, Hilary seated herself in the chair he had cleaned for her.

'And now,' said Marcus, leaning against the table so that he was half sitting and half standing, 'I can tell you everything.' His voice had roughened.

Hilary felt her heart begin to beat more quickly as he took her hands.

'Hilary, I have wonderful news. I never thought anything could resolve the difficulties that stood between us, but I was wrong. I have learnt the truth about my birth and it has set me free. When I went to Lyme, I visited my mother's old nurse. She told me that I was not tainted by madness; that I was free to marry. Hilary, I am not Lord Carisbrooke's son.'

She was perplexed. 'What do you mean? Of course, you are Lord Carisbrooke's son. That is why you inherited the title.'

'No. I am not related to him in any way.'

Briefly, he told her what he had learnt in Lyme.

'Then if you are not Lord Carisbrooke's son . . .' she said slowly, hope dawning in her breast as she began to understand.

He waited patiently, whilst she took in the full implication of what he had said.

'. . . then you have not inherited his madness.'

'No.'

'Marcus, this is wonderful news.'

'It is. Because it allows me to do this.' He took her hands in his. 'And this.' He kissed her. 'And it allows me to ask you the question I have been burning to ask you ever since I learnt the truth.

Hilary, will you marry me?'

She looked him full in the face, and there was a moment of profound connection between them.

'Yes, Marcus, I will,' she said softly.

He kissed her on the lips. Then he pulled away.

'No more,' he said. 'Otherwise I will not be able to stop. The wedding will be at once – that is, unless you have any objection?' he asked.

'No,' she reassured him. 'None.'

He smiled. 'I hoped you would not have. As soon as we escape from here and restore Esmerelda to Mrs Lund's care I will set about acquiring a special licence, and we will be married without delay. It means you will have to wait for your wedding clothes—'

'As to that, I don't need any wedding clothes,' she interrupted.

'Oh, yes you do. I want to see you in gowns that will bring out your full beauty, instead of those dreadful sacks you wear.'

He was teasing her, and she smiled. However, she was under no illusions about her personal charms.

'I am no beauty,' she said.

His voice softened and his eyes became liquid pools. 'You are to me.'

Hilary melted. There was such a note of sincerity in his voice that she knew that what he said was true. She might be little, and mousy and plain, but to him she was beautiful. She gave a sigh of pure pleasure. It was more than she had ever hoped for; more than she had ever dared dream.

'I will buy you a ruby silk—'

'You will do nothing of the sort,' she said, laughing. 'I would feel like a stranger in such a dress. But I confess I would like a change from my usual gowns. Some nice neat muslin.' She gave an embarrassed smile. 'It is foolish of me, I know, but I have always had a fancy for primrose.'

He smiled. 'Then you shall have it. A primrose muslin, a primrose satin, a primrose silk . . . .'

One of the candles sputtered and went out, breaking in on their happy thoughts and reminding them of the reality of their situation.

Hilary sobered.

'I had not realized we had been in here so long,' she said, as she saw how far down the other candles had burnt. 'If they should go out . . . .'

She gave a shiver. Then frowned, as she remembered another time when she had been trapped. It had not been dark then. It had been daylight. But the two incidents bore similar hallmarks.

'This reminds me of the time I was locked on the roof,' she said. 'Did you ever ask the Lunds about it?'

He nodded. 'I did. But neither of them locked the door.'

Hilary thought. 'Could it have been Esmerelda who locked me out?' she asked, thinking it possible that Esmerelda had done so if she had been loose.

He shook his head. 'No. Again, I asked the Lunds. She was safely in the cottage when it occurred.'

Hilary's thoughts wandered down other channels. She had wondered at the time whether either of the Palmers could have locked her out on the roof. But even if they had done so, they could not be behind her present predicament as they were no longer at the abbey. And even if, by some chance, either one of them had visited the abbey that day, then although they might have had a reason for shutting her in, they could have had no reason for shutting Marcus in. No, it must be Esmerelda who had trapped them, as Marcus suspected.

Hilary gave a sigh. She was growing tired of being trapped.

She began to set her thoughts to work.

'When we came in here,' she said a few minutes later, 'into this room, the passageway leading to it continued a little further. If I remember the plans rightly, the outside of the abbey must lie in that direction, and it cannot be far away. What if the passage leads to another door?'

'Unfortunately it doesn't. The passage continues for another ten feet or so, and then it is blocked.'

'With what?'

'Rocks, soil . . .' he said.

'Has it always been blocked?'

'Yes, ever since I can remember it.' He became thoughtful. 'Still, it could once have formed a way out, I suppose. It would have provided the priest with an escape route if the room had been discovered.'

'Then I suggest we take a look. If the passage continues beyond the blockage then we might be able to find another exit.'

Marcus picked up his branched candlestick. Taking her hand, he led her out of the priest's hole and together they followed the passage to its end. A pile of wood, soil and stone blocked the way.

Marcus handed her the candelabra. She held it steady whilst he began to move the wood blockage to one side. To begin with he revealed nothing but more detritus. Then he gave a satisfied exclamation.

'What is it?' asked Hilary.

'I think there might be a way through after all. I'm not sure, but I think there's a door.'

He threw more stones aside, and before long a door had been revealed.

Hilary's hopes soared. They would soon be free!

Marcus tried the handle and pushed. It moved a little . . . then stopped.

'There must be something behind it,' he said.

Hilary's spirits fell. To be so close to escape, and yet so far . . . .

But Marcus had not given up. He set his shoulder to the door and heaved. The door began to give.

'It's moving,' he said. 'Another few heaves and it should give way.'

He set his shoulder to the door again, and before very many minutes had passed he had managed to open it enough to step through.

Hilary felt a faint stirring of air.

'We were right!' She smiled. 'It leads outside.'

She put her hand protectively around the candle flames, which were flickering with the sudden draught.

'I'll go first,' said Marcus.

Reclaiming his candelabra he stepped through the door and went down the newly revealed passageway. Hilary followed at his heels, only to find it ended in a wall of earth.

Marcus cursed.

He stood and thought. 'It doesn't make sense. There must be a way out. There'd be no point in having a passage here otherwise. And the fresh air must be coming from somewhere.'

He pressed the walls, but they were solid. Then he looked up.

'Aha.'

Set in to the roof of the passage was a circle of wood.

He reached up and pushed it. It gave slightly. He pushed again, and then heaved it up and aside. Daylight flooded in.

Hilary felt a surge in her spirits. After so long trapped in the dark, it was wonderful to be free. She breathed in deeply, rejoicing in the fresh air and the feel of the wind on her cheek.

She turned to Marcus, and his smile answered her own.

He took her hand, his long fingers stroking her palm. The feel was companionable and comforting.

After allowing their eyes to adjust to the light, Marcus blew out the candles. Setting his candelabra aside he made a step with his hands.

'Come,' he said to Hilary. 'I will help you up.'

She needed no second bidding. She was eager to be free of the dark, dank tunnel, and setting down her own candlestick she placed her foot in his clasped hands so that he could raise her up. Once her head and shoulders had emerged, she looked about her. The scene was a familiar one. All around her were ivy-clad stones.

'We're in the folly,' she said.

The ruined temple had never seemed more welcoming.

She put her palms down flat on the earth and, with Marcus pushing from below, she pulled herself out.

She straightened up and brushed the dirt from her pelisse, then resettled her bonnet, which had been knocked askew, and looked around her once again. She had actually emerged in the middle of the folly. Beyond it she could see the tangled shrubbery, and in the distance the abbey.

She stepped aside from the hole, giving Marcus room to follow her.

He caught at the sides and pulled himself up, his great height allowing him to climb out without help.

As they stood once more in the daylight, above the ground, Hilary felt a rush of elation. They had escaped!

Marcus joined her in her exclamations of relief.

'We'll return to the abbey at once,' he said. 'We'll go by way of the cottage. If Esmerelda has tired of playing, she might well have gone back there of her own accord.'

'And if not?' asked Hilary.

'Then we must look for her. It is not safe to leave her on her own.'

Hilary nodded. Overjoyed though she was to be betrothed to Marcus, and to have escaped their terrifying predicament, she knew they would not be able to rest until Esmerelda had been found.

Marcus took her hand, and together they went through the grounds. They moved cautiously in case they came across Esmerelda on the way, but there was no sign of her. They came to the track leading to the cottage and looked down its length. The door of the cottage was closed.

'That's odd,' said Marcus. He dropped Hilary's hand. 'Wait here,' he said.

He approached the door warily.

Hilary was glad of his caution, for there was a noise coming from inside.

'Esmerelda?' called Marcus softly.

To Hilary's surprise, it was not Esmerelda's voice that answered him. It was Lund's.

'Your lordship?' came Lund's cracked tones.

'Lund?' asked Marcus in astonishment.

'Heaven be praised!' said Lund. 'It's Lady Esmerelda. She's locked me in.'

Marcus drew back the bolt on the outside of the door and Lund emerged from the cottage, looking distressed.

'How did this happen?' asked Marcus.

'I don't rightly know,' said Lund, shaking his head. 'I came out to the cottage to take care of Lady Esmerelda whilst Mrs Lund brought the last of her things from the room behind the tapestry, but when I got here I found the door already open. I put my head round it, cautious like, and someone pushed me inside, then bolted the door behind me.'

'Esmerelda must have found another way out.'

'I don't see how she can have done. I checked the cottage myself.'

'Well, no matter. We have other, more important things to think about,' said Marcus. 'Such as finding Esmerelda. You begin searching the grounds, Lund. We have come from the folly, and she is not there, but she might have gone down to the river. The bridge has always been a favourite haunt of hers. Caesar is also missing. He might be with Esmerelda, so listen for his bark. Miss Wentworth and

I will search the abbey. If we can find Mrs Lund, she can help us in our search, too.'

Lund departed, heading for the river.

Marcus took Hilary's hand once more and they continued on their way to the abbey. In the fading light it seemed menacing. Its gaunt architecture promised no respite from their troubles.

Hilary shivered.

She had no idea what they were going to find when they went inside.

CHAPTER THIRTEEN

*H*ilary and Marcus stood for a minute outside the door. But they knew they could not delay.

'Courage,' said Marcus.

Hilary nodded.

They passed through the heavy oak door and into the hall.

'I am going to search downstairs first,' said Marcus. 'If Esmerelda shut the secret door she might well be in the drawing-room waiting for us to emerge, so that is where I am going to begin.'

'I'll come with you,' said Hilary.

'No. I want you to remain here. She might not be in the drawing-room. She might be in the kitchens, or up in the attics, and I don't want her to be able to slip out of the abbey without our being aware of it. If you remain in the hall, then she cannot leave without you seeing her. If you do, call me, but don't try to stop her yourself, not even if she is making for the door. She is stronger than she looks, and she will not hesitate to harm you if you get in her way.'

Hilary did not protest. She had seen too much of Esmerelda's madness to disagree.

'I won't be long,' he said.

He disappeared in the direction of the drawing-room.

It was cold in the hall. The fire had burned down low. Hilary would have liked to hold her hands out to the glowing embers, but she did not want to turn her back on the hall. The cavernous space seemed threatening. In the fading light it was full of shadows. Any one of them could hide Esmerelda.

She set her back to the fireplace and stood looking outwards, so that she could not be taken by surprise.

Several times her eyes played tricks on her, telling her that there was someone in the dark recess under the galleried landing, hiding behind one of the suits of armour. But there was no one there.

She heard noises, too. A creaking sound, which turned out to be the drawing-room door as Marcus opened it, and a tapping, which was nothing more than the sound of his footsteps, greatly magnified, crossing the stone hall.

He returned after a few minutes to tell her that he could not find Esmerelda in any of the main rooms, and that he was going down to search the kitchens.

'She has fond memories of them dating from her childhood,' said Marcus. 'She might well have gone there.'

His footsteps faded away again.

Hilary pulled her pelisse more closely around herself and tried to calm her nerves.

A few minutes later she heard a sound from above.

She looked up, fearing to see Esmerelda on the landing . . . but instead, she saw Mr Ulverstone.

She was astonished. What was Mr Ulverstone doing there?

Whatever it was, she must warn him of his danger. If Esmerelda was upstairs . . . .

She moved towards the staircase and began to ascend.

At that moment he looked down and saw her, and a look of pure anger spread across his face.

'How did you escape?' he demanded, his brow thunderous.

His words were so unexpected that she did not immediately take them in. She had been expecting him to say, 'What are you doing at the abbey?' or, 'Miss Wentworth, I did not expect you find you here.' But instead he had said, How did you *escape*.

But how did he know that she had been trapped? Unless . . . unless *he had been the one to trap her.*

But why would he do such a thing?

She had no time to think about it, for he started to walk along the landing, towards the stairs.

'You seem to make a habit of escaping from perilous situations,' he said.

At his words, Hilary's thoughts flew back to another perilous situation, when she had been trapped on the roof, and the light of understanding dawned.

'It was you who locked me out,' she gasped.

'Of course. Why else do you think I would ignore your shouts and waves when you tried to attract my attention as I crossed the stable yard? If it hadn't been me, I would have sprung to your assistance.'

So he had seen her after all.

'But why?' she asked, beginning to retreat backwards down the stairs without taking her eyes from him.

She had suspected the Palmers of being involved because they had had a motive for removing her, but she could not think why Mr Ulverstone should want to do her harm.

'Why? To prevent you getting too close to Marcus, of course. I'd seen him kissing you in the library, and I knew that he was falling in love with you, but a marriage between the two of you did not suit my plans.'

'Plans?' Hilary felt herself go cold and for a moment she stopped edging backwards. 'What plans?'

'To inherit. And to that end, Marcus had to die childless – not with a wife, and a child on the way. I'd already tried to prevent such a situation arising by asking you to marry me – even before I saw the two of you embracing in the library, I could tell that Marcus was

attracted to you – but that hadn't worked, so I had to use more dras-
tic means. I was just wondering what to do when I saw you heading
towards the attic and decided to follow you. When you climbed out
on the roof it was too good an opportunity to miss. If I locked you
out, I could be rid of you without anyone suspecting foul play. As the
door is old and it sticks, your entrapment on the roof and subsequent
death would have been regarded as an accident, for I would have
unlocked the door the following morning to remove all suspicion of
anything else. It's just a pity Marcus found you. Otherwise I could
have been rid of you permanently.'

'Are you really so envious of his title that you would go to such
lengths to make sure you remain his heir?' asked Hilary, edging backwards once again down another stair.

'His title?' Mr Ulverstone laughed. 'I don't want his title. I never
wanted his title. I want his money.'

And then a couple of memories flashed suddenly before Hilary's
mind's eye, memories she had never before connected but which
now seemed to have a terrible logic. Mr Ulverstone's casual remark
that fortunes could be won or lost on the turn of a card, and the
names of *Howard and Gibbs* that had been scrawled on the back of
the card he had given her. Howard and Gibbs. She remembered who
they were now.

'You were in the clutches of the moneylenders,' she said out loud.
'You've lost your fortune. You lost it on a game of cards.'

'My, my, you are sharp. Yes. I lost everything at White's. Two
hundred thousand pounds on the turn of a card. I thought my hand
was unbeatable, but I was wrong.'

'So you had to raise money in order to pay your gambling debt,
and now you can't pay back the loan,' said Hilary, seeing how it must
have been.

'You're sharp,' he said appraisingly, 'but not sharp enough. You're
right when you say I had to raise a loan to pay the debt, but wrong

to say I can't pay it back. I can. Just as soon as I've disposed of Marcus.'

And Hilary saw it all. Mr Ulverstone was Marcus's heir. And . . . 'You mean to kill him,' she gasped.

'I do.' He stood at the top of the stairs, looking down at her. 'Once he's out of the way the money will be mine.'

'But I still don't understand how you came here,' she said, perplexed. 'You were going to London. I saw you leave the abbey.'

He sneered. 'I took the Palmers home, but as for going to London, that was nothing but a tale. I spent the night at a nearby inn and returned to the abbey on horseback the following day, only to see Marcus's coach leaving. I bribed one of the stablehands to tell me when he returned, then went back to the inn. As luck would have it, I saw him return myself, when his coach rolled past the inn. By riding across country I was able to reach the abbey before him.'

'But why trap him in the passage?'

'Marcus is much larger than I am. An open attack would not succeed. But I knew he'd venture into the passage if he thought Esmerelda had escaped, and going without food and water will kill even the strongest man: with one end blocked, and the lever broken at the other, the passage was a death trap.'

So that would have been Marcus's fate if they had not escaped. And, because she had inconveniently returned to the abbey, it would also have been hers.

'I'm surprised you had the courage to do it yourself,' said Hilary scathingly.

'I must confess I thought of hiring someone, but underlings can be so unreliable. Besides, I enjoyed doing it myself. Or would have done, if you hadn't escaped. Still, there's more than one way to commit murder,' he said. 'You should have accepted my hand whilst you had the chance. I would have taken you to London and abandoned you there, but you would have been alive. Now you know too much.'

Reaching beneath his tailcoat he pulled out a knife.

Hilary felt her palms grow damp.

She was nearly at the bottom of the staircase, and once she had reached it she knew she would have to turn and run.

But just as she was about to edge down the last two stairs, she caught a sight of movement behind him. It was a ghostly figure, dressed all in white.

'Esmerelda!'

'Oh, no, you don't distract me like that,' he sneered. 'Esmerelda's playing with Caesar – poor hound! She's been very useful, one way or another. Particularly when I gave her a knife and left her in the drawing-room to wait for you. It wasn't her fault that she didn't manage to kill you. She certainly tried hard enough. And to think, at one time I tried to persuade Marcus to put her in an asylum! If I'd managed to convince him, then this whole plan would have been impossible. I could still have killed Marcus, of course, but I would-n't have had a ready made scapegoat to hand.'

'So that's why you freed her.'

'I needed someone to blame, and who better than a madwoman? Even better, a dead madwoman – the dead tell no tales. She would have been in the river by now, like her father, but she ran off. Never mind, she can wait.'

He raised the knife – and then a plaintive cry stopped him in his tracks. 'Laurence!'

Hilary saw his startled look, before he turned to face Esmerelda.

The mad young woman was walking towards him along the land-ing with a purposeful air.

'Esmerelda.' His voice wavered. 'I thought you were playing with Caesar in the tapestry room.'

'Caesar didn't want to play,' she said sulkily.

'Never mind,' said Mr Ulverstone, recovering from his shock and walking towards her along the landing, away from his precarious position at the top of the stairs. 'Why don't we go and find Marcus? I'm sure he'll want to play.'

'I don't want to play with Marcus,' she said. 'I want to play with the knife.'

'Now, Esmerelda,' he said, his voice trembling, 'this isn't yours.'

Hilary watched in horror as Esmerelda closed on him and the two of them grappled for possession of the knife. It should have been an uneven contest, for he was a man and she was a woman, but she had the strength of the mad.

The struggle became more desperate. It carried them backwards and forwards and across the landing, to the wall, to the banister . . . .

Hilary stood frozen to the spot.

They were leaning over the banister now. Mr Ulverstone was being pressed further and further back, locked in a life-or-death struggle with Esmerelda, overbalancing, toppling, falling . . . .

'No!'

The cry was torn from Hilary as the two combatants plunged from the landing. She froze as she watched them fall. They seemed to spend an eternity in mid air before landing with a sickening series of cracks on the stone-flagged floor.

And then there was nothing.

Hilary stood in shocked silence, trying to take it all in. And then slowly, as her limbs came back under her control she went back down the stairs and across the hall. The two bodies, lying twisted on the floor, looked like broken dolls. She knelt down beside them.

Her heart was filled with pity as she felt for Esmerelda's pulse and discovered that the beautiful, mad young woman was dead.

And Mr Ulverstone, the architect of the tragedy. He, too, was dead.

Hilary began to shiver.

She drew away from the bodies. She turned . . . to see Marcus striding towards her across the hall. And then he was beside her, and she leant against him, feeling his strong arms close round her as she buried her face in his chest.

'I'm so sorry,' she said, when she had at last recovered herself and lifted her head.

'Hush, my dearest. It's all right.'

'It was your cousin . . .'

'I know. I was there.'

She looked at him questioningly.

'I found Mrs Lund locked in the kitchen, and together we searched the basement. When we found nothing, she went to help Lund outside, slipping out of the kitchen door. I intended to continue my search for Esmerelda upstairs, and arrived in the hall in time to see everything.'

'Then you know it all.'

'Yes.'

'I should have done something,' said Hilary.

'Hush, my love, there was nothing you could do. And if you had tried to intervene, matters might have been worse. You might have fallen, too.'

Hilary nodded. She knew what he said was true.

'Come. You're shivering,' he said. 'This has been a terrible shock.'

He guided her through into the library and sat her in front of the fire, then sat down beside her. The embers of the fire were glowing and gave out some welcome heat.

'So it was Laurence who was behind the attacks on you,' he said. 'And Laurence who freed Esmerelda. And, of course, it was Laurence who locked the Lunds in so that they could not worry about Esmerelda's absence, or mine, and begin a search. I wonder if he meant to kill them, too?'

'I don't think he cared about them,' sighed Hilary. 'Whether they lived or died was unimportant to him. It was your death he cared about. I only hope he didn't imprison the outdoor staff as well.'

'I think it unlikely. They often go for days without seeing either myself or the Lunds, so they would not have been a threat to his plan. By the time they'd noticed my absence, I would have already been dead.'

He fell silent.

Hilary knew he was thinking of Esmerelda. He had loved her as a brother should, and had tried to protect her from the consequences of her own madness. He had kept her at the abbey, where she could be cared for kindly by people who loved her, and although she had caused him a great deal of anguish, Hilary knew he was devastated by her death.

'And so it is over,' said Marcus at last. 'We are both safe. But at what a cost.'

They held each other close, taking mutual comfort from their embrace.

'And what of Caesar?' asked Hilary, wondering how high the cost had been. 'Did you see him when you searched the abbey, or . . .' She did not like to suggest an alternative. If Esmerelda had been *playing* with him, he might be injured, or dead.

But at the mention of his name there came a slight noise from behind the curtains and a minute later Caesar emerged.

'He must have taken refuge in here when Esmerelda started teasing him!' she said with a smile, as the hound padded over to them. After all the terrible events of the afternoon, it seemed a good omen to see him alive and in one piece.

He stretched and yawned, just as though nothing momentous had happened. The normality of his behaviour did much to restore Hilary's spirits. It had been a terrifying time but at last it was over.

Caesar nudged her hand with his head.

She stroked his soft fur, and scratched him behind the ears. He wagged his tail appreciatively, then settled down at her feet.

Then Marcus roused himself. They had had a brief respite from horror, but now its consequences must be faced.

'The next few weeks will not be pleasant ones, I'm afraid,' he said, as he stood up.

'I know,' she assured him. 'Two people are dead. There will inevitably be consequences.'

He took her hand. 'I will send Lund for Sir Giles Routledge. He is the local magistrate.'

'Are you not the magistrate?' she asked in surprise.

He shook his head. 'I never wanted that particular duty. It would have involved a lot of people coming and going at the abbey,' he explained, 'and with Esmerelda in a fragile state I did not want that to happen. But Sir Giles is a fair man. He will handle everything with discretion and tact.' He stood up. 'I must find the Lunds. I will return as soon as possible.'

Hilary nodded.

Once he had left the room, she fell to stroking Caesar again. Although she was not looking forward to the aftermath of that terrible afternoon she knew she could face it, because she would not be alone. She and Marcus would face it together.

EPILOGUE

A tragic accident.

Hilary gave a sigh as she read the lettering on Esmerelda's gravestone.

It was hard to believe it was now more than five years since that fateful day in 1810 when Esmerelda and Laurence had plunged to their deaths. Hilary's thoughts were dark as she remembered it in all its terrible detail: the note she had received from Marcus, telling her to meet him at the abbey; their entrapment in the secret passage; their escape; and their discovery that Laurence had been the instrument of their captivity.

Her thoughts moved on, to the moment she had seen Laurence on the landing, and had seen Esmerelda behind him. She remembered the way he had struggled with the mad young woman, and the way they had plunged to the hall below.

Other memories were less clear. Lund going to fetch Sir Giles Routledge, and Sir Giles's deduction that the deaths had been accidental: knowing that Esmerelda had been ill for some time, and assuming like everyone else in the neighbourhood that her sickness had been of the body and not the mind, he had listened to Lund's garbled account of the tragedy on the way back to the abbey and by the time he had arrived he had decided that Esmerelda must have felt faint whilst on the landing; that Laurence had sprung to her assistance; and that in an attempt to prevent her from toppling over the banister he had overbalanced himself and the two of them had fallen to their deaths.

The knife, the one piece of evidence that might have suggested a different interpretation, had not been found by Sir Giles. It had been dropped by Esmerelda in the struggle, and had fallen behind one of the suits of armour beneath the stairs.

And so the matter had been officially regarded as a tragic accident and the case had been closed.

Then had come the aftermath: Esmerelda's funeral; the winding up of Laurence's affairs; and Laurence's funeral in London, which had been generously arranged by Marcus.

And after the darkness, a chance for love.

Yes, love.

Hilary's thoughts brightened as she arranged the flowers she had brought to the grave. She put them in the container and their gay colours showed up delightfully against the stone.

It was love that had saved them.

It had saved both her and Marcus during the dark days following Esmerelda's death, and it had nourished and sustained them as they had come to terms with the tragedy. And then, as the memory of the horror had receded, that same love had grown and blossomed, becoming a source of great joy and fruitfulness.

The five years since then had been the most wonderful she had ever known. She had married Marcus in a quiet ceremony, attended only by his mother's old nurse, Maud, her sister, Yvonne, and Mr and Mrs Lund. Then she and Marcus had gone to Bath. They had visited his mother's friend, then spent a quiet month healing their bodies and their minds before returning to the abbey.

Through the long winter months that had followed they had jointly planned its restoration, and over the summer the work had begun. The venerable old building had come back to life, its smaller rooms being rescued from the dust sheets whilst the larger ones had been entirely refurbished.

She heard Marcus approaching.

'Are you ready to go back to the abbey, my love?' he asked.

'I am.'

He slipped his arm around her waist and together they walked back to the venerable old building. The grounds had taken on a brighter aspect over the last few years. The shrubs had been neatly pruned, and an array of colourful summer flowers had been planted beneath them. The lawns had been tidied, the grass had been cut short and its edges neatened.

As they approached the abbey, the rich colours of the stained glass windows glowed like jewels in the sunshine, winking and shining from afar. Even the spires and points seemed to have lost their gauntness, and had taken on a new beauty in the summer sunshine.

Hilary and Marcus went inside. The hall now exuded cheerfulness. The tables flanking the fireplace were highly polished, and the fresh flowers arranged in ornate vases on top of them were filling the air with their delicious perfume.

The weapons had been removed from their place above the fireplace, and the suits of armour had gone. The hall had lost its warlike appearance, and was now bright and homely.

They went through into the drawing-room. Hilary's gaze swept over the brightly polished windows, the damask cutains and newly upholstered furniture, then came to rest on four-year-old Harry, who was playing with Caesar by the window. Beside him sat two-year-old Elizabeth, and on the rug lay little Thomas.

'Have the children been good?' she asked Mrs Lund, who was sitting by the window sewing.

'Very good,' Mrs Lund smiled.

Hilary looked at her two older children fondly, then went over to the baby, who was kicking his pudgy legs in the air. She picked him up and carried him over to his father.

Marcus took the baby and cradled him in his arms.

'Until you came here I used to think the abbey was cursed,' he said, kissing the baby on top of his head.

Hilary's eyes once more swept the peaceful scene, drinking in the sight of the children playing in a shaft of sunlight; Mrs Lund looking peaceful and serene; and the beautifully restored drawing-room.

She rested her head on Marcus's shoulder.

'No, it isn't cursed,' she said, with a sigh of deep contentment. 'It's blessed.'